Rook's Hill

Ghost Tales From A Hidden World

Rook's Hill

Ghost Tales From A Hidden World

Rosemary Pavey

The Midnight Oil Artisan Press

2018

Cover illustration and design by Rosemary Pavey

The Midnight Oil Artisan Press
www.paveypenandpaint.com

Printed by Createspace

ISBN: 978-0-9927463-5-3

*This book is for all who appreciate
the secret life of Things.*

*We are surrounded by hidden worlds.
The Past, the Future, the Imagined,
the Might-have-been... A writer forever
has one ear at the door, listening for
echoes from such places, so is it any
wonder that stories often provide our
nearest approach to the 'unknown'?
Mystery is our natural element and
never do we feel it more than when a
fireside tale stirs up a shiver or two...*

*Warm inside – dark outside:
the human condition in a nutshell.*

Acknowledgement

My grateful thanks to those who have helped me in the creation of this book and without whose patience and goodwill nothing could have been accomplished. My particular thanks to Richard Alford and Michael Alford who provided background information for 'The Chenoo' and 'White Lead' respectively.
Any errors throughout are definitely my own.

Quotations

p. 61 *Sohrab and Rustum* ll.721-723 by Matthew Arnold.
p.105: *The Egyptian Book of the Dead*
Ch. CXXV after the translation by E.A. Wallis Budge, 1895.
p.135 *The Birks of Aberfeldy* l.1 by Robert Burns

The Author

Rosemary Pavey was born in 1960 and works as a writer and painter in Sussex, dividing her time between her studio at the Turner Dumbrell Workshops, Ditchling, and Stoneywish Nature Reserve.

Also by Rosemary Pavey

The Beehive Cluster - *A Novel for all Ages*
The Magpie's Nest - *A Summer School*
Christmas Ghosties - *Tales for a Winter Night*

Forthcoming Titles

Painting and Chaos
A Cuckoo in Hell

These titles are available from www.Amazon.com and Amazon.co.uk or direct from the author's website and gallery. To find out more about any of these or exhibitions, talks and other events, please visit:
www.paveypenandpaint.com

Contents

Rook's Hill

For Gillie and Kimmy
in memory of a morning excursion

Rook's Hill

The day we found Rook's Hill is etched upon my mind, as vivid as a childhood memory. It was a blue-and-white, sky-lark day - Dutch clouds frothing over the Weald - and we had been walking on the Downs, ankle deep in hawksbit and nodding scabius flowers, heading for Tegbury Beacon. That was a particularly fine year for butterflies, as I recall, and the chalkhill blues and early skippers were already abundant. Rook's Hill, according to the guide books, had a reputation for ghosts and apparitions. Five men were hanged there in the 1730s - felons of the days when smugglers regularly took the sunken track heading north from the sea. A group of wind-torn beeches, known as the Five Brothers, later commemorated their fate. Whenever one blew down, it was the local custom to plant another. But legend had also taken root there and it was said that if you wanted to meet the Devil, you had only to put your shoes on the wrong feet and run backwards round the trees on a moonlit night.

Such fancies seemed a world away that summer day. We had eaten our sandwiches in a hollow and stretched out on the grass, watching the kestrels as they hunted, threaded on the wind beneath us. Beyond them lay the picture-book village of Felping. We could make out the church, with its grey, hooded tower, tucked among the trees. And at the foot of the bostal - the old shepherd's path which joined the smuggler's track - stood The Fountain Inn. A spring gushed from the chalk nearby and the lane was lined with cars, affirming the enduring popularity of their Cartwheel Pies (*Rookie Pies* they called them, though everyone knew they were chicken). Whatever their authenticity, these pies made the perfect accompaniment to a much-vaunted range of aromatic beers and the day trippers could never get enough of either. After the pub came a patchwork of browns and greens, the scarcely-distinguishable tints of rooftop and garden, but our eyes were drawn to something set apart - a teeny, white cottage, clinging to the hem of the hill.

3

Perhaps we were tempted by curiosity, perhaps prompted by an unrecognised shiver as the shadows of the 'Brothers' beside us began to lengthen. However it was, we decided to abandon our original route, leave the ridge and explore the underhill. We tramped down, singing with the exuberance of walkers who are easy in their stride. We had covered six miles already and if we did no more than retrace our steps we would still notch up a creditable day's march. Moreover, we had the whole afternoon ahead of us and as we folded our maps away we experienced a delightful sense of freedom. This was more fun than following a route. This was proper stepping out - trusting the moment, like the kestrels on their invisible thermals, for there are updraughts which affect the earthbound too, currents of energy, constantly flowing through our lives and those who ride them, living from moment to moment, enjoy the thrill of chance without expense of effort. Such unseen energies cut through the common boundaries of time and space. They are truly creative.

At the bottom of the hill, we emerged by the cottage we had seen and now we could tell it was not one place, but two. Whereas one side dozed and winked in the afternoon sun, the other was buzzing with life. Built with their backs towards the village, like excommunicants, they had the whole span of the downs before them. What better place for watching out for travellers from the south - a wink of light, an outlaw's signal - a line of laden ponies - any romance imagination could supply? Summer roses romped along the wall of the second cottage and formed a wayward hedge through which we glimpsed a lawn, neatly divided by a brick-paved path. There was a statue and tubs of lavender. The windows nestled beneath an ageing thatch. A party was in progress. The front door stood ajar and groups of visitors passed casually in and out and sauntered in the garden, sipping wine.

"Can we tempt you in?" asked a diminutive red-head by the gate. "It's Open House today. The more the merrier." Not waiting for a reply, she thrust a glass in my hand and gave a smile. "I'm Letitia. The book stall is through there, in the cottage. Refreshments in the kitchen and there's another garden to explore around the back. Don't worry about your boots!" She was thirty, perhaps, garbed in copper coloured harem-pants and a cream, cashmere chemise. She dripped jewellery - silver and turquoise, mostly. Her casual curls were bound with a scarf - expensive - real silk - eau-de-nil. It was all very bohemian. Oblivious to our embarrassment, she waved us through and we, intrigued by the novelty of it all, exchanged uncertain smiles and tiptoed in.

The craze for Open Houses was just then at its height. Every self-respecting village boasted its own Craft or Culture Festival, while 'makers' who made anything at all, threw open their doors to the public in the hope of making a little money too. Painters, sculptors, potters, quilters, glass-blowers and withy-weavers all set up exhibitions of their own. There seemed no end to the variety of skills on offer and one could spend a pleasant week or two, under pretext of viewing the Art, taking a gratifying peek at each venue's plumbing and landscape design. *Have you visited the loo at No.6? They have gold-plated taps in the bathroom. And isn't the gazebo at No.12 to die for?*

Mouse Cottage (we spotted the name, half hidden by flowering jasmine) was a perfect example of its type: the furnishings modern; the art severely abstract; both sitting easily within its ancient walls. Floors, windows, ceilings, sloped in a deliciously random way. You could hardly stand straight without hitting your head on a beam, yet everything else, arranged with understated care, bore the signature of contemporary chic. Money too. Nothing had been spared to create the perfect ambience. And books... Well, it hardly surprised us to learn that the owner was an author. We had, as we later learnt, stumbled upon a literary launch

"'Fraid you've missed the reading," said a man in a silk-lined jacket. He was handing out canapés - prawns with parsley and sesame toasts - offering a quip and a smile to each guest in turn.

"Sorry?"

"Letitia. She was reading from her latest. Have you come down specially for the signing?"

He implied that we must be from London, and, not wishing to disappoint him I was minded to answer 'yes'. Would it matter that we had only 'come down' from the hill?

"Such a pity her new agent could not be here. Of course, he's the one who has made all the difference. She was going through a rough patch before. Almost gave up writing altogether. It's the devil, isn't it, writer's block? Have you suffered from it much? What kind of thing do you do?"

Feeling like frauds, we prudently edged away, but Letitia caught up with us again in the conservatory. She seemed determined to make everyone personally welcome. And she was so natural, so interested in others' affairs. She made us feel that she really cared what we thought and where we had come from and *had* we tried the pissaladière?

She led us on a tour of the garden, pointing out favourite shrubs. She had been here for six months and couldn't *believe* her luck in finding such a darling place to live. The garden was a labour of love and as for the setting... Every day she walked on the downs, she said. Sunrise. Sunset. Seeing the world from the top had become something of an obsession. Up there the words just came to her and down here she could wrap herself in solitude and write to her heart's content. Nice people in the village, too, and the station only three miles away.

Bliss. It was in the air that afternoon amongst the visitors, the bee-heavy borage flowers. It was thick, almost palpable. The cottage hummed with it. How could we resist? We let it enfold us and bought her book - a supernatural romance, not our kind of thing at all. We never read it, of course, and I have no idea what eventually became of it. Most probably, it went to a charity shop. But Felping - Felping long remained in our minds as a picture of paradise. Whenever skies were grey and the dreary roof-scape of Brighton hemmed us in, we would make a mental journey and pitch our dreams in the white cottage under Rook's Hill. The moon came up on those dreams and the snow fell round them. We furnished them with our own chairs and tables. We took imagined breakfast in the garden, snuggled up to winter fires, and listened, enchanted, as the bells rang out for practice from the church tower down the lane. The power of invention enriched our restricted lives. How else could we have endured the frustration of being poor and without prospect? Hemmed about on every side by urban monotony, how could we even have breathed without the Downs as our virtual lungs? And we had made such a habit of this parallel living, had invested Felping with so much of the magic of desire, a physical return seemed inadvisable. Better to keep our golden memories intact...

That was until one December afternoon. I was idling at the computer, looking for winter scenes to enliven the round-robin letter I always send at Christmas-time: *This year we biked around Normandy. Philip got onto the company football team. I joined a knitting group. We treated ourselves to a bungee-jump for our wedding anniversary...* In retrospect, our achievements sounded dull. I might as well have said: *We tramped the paths marked out for us by an indifferent Fate: this milestone, that milestone, so many steps taken, so many the less to go.* We were still stuck in our city flat. Still buying lottery tickets - not that we believed we would win - we were simply afraid to let our numbers go. Philip is a statistician. Notwithstanding that fact, he shared with me the irrational belief that the numbers, having a secret life of their own, would turn up trumps for somebody else if given half a chance.

Here, on the screen, one image caught my eye. Huddled beneath an impending moon, were the Five Brothers, conspiring on Rook's Hill. There was no mistaking them. Their naked arms beckoned towards the Weald. *Did you ever wonder how the world looks when you are not there to see? We know,* they whispered, and the moon confirmed it, *we could tell you what lies on the hidden side.* Of course, the moon would understand about all that, *wouldn't* she? And instantly that was what *I* most urgently needed to know. Even as a tiny cluster of pixels, the trees exerted a fatal magnetism. I felt the wind lift beneath my thoughts and carry them, unresisting, to the narrow path from which the picture was taken.

Two taps on my touchpad opened up the listings page of a well-known property agent. "*Birdsong and blackberries...*" ran the heading. "*Moonrise and morning dew.*" This was a novel ploy: selling dreams through words, under the banner of 'Beautiful Sussex'. But the text itself set my heart off at a canter:

"Mouse Cottage. Felping. Set in one of the most romantic situations in the South. Two bedrooms, shower room, reception

room, kitchen, 2 w.c's. Bijou garden. Conservatory. Parking. Stunning uninterrupted views of the Downs. OIRO £400,000. Quick sale desirable.

"Public Viewing Dec. 21st at 11.00 a.m."

"It's for sale!" I shouted. "Philip, come and look! *Our* cottage. It's up for sale!"

Already my imagination was in a ferment, devising impractical schemes for raising cash. We could sell the flat, the car, cash in our paltry pensions... Perhaps my mother would advance us a loan? Perhaps this week the lottery... If only some unknown relative could do us the kindness of shuffling off and leave us a bequest...

"We could go and *see* it," I urged, dismissing former doubts. "No harm in *that*. Just think how pretty the place would look under a blanket of snow... We could express an interest, even if we had to pull out later on. I could telephone..."

No need to say what Philip's answer was. On the shortest day of the year, we set out for our rendez-vous. It was a still, grey, silent day. Dripping hedgerows dangled the last haw-berries, like old blood-clots, from tangled boughs. Cold, sad horses stood in the fields in their cumbersome winter coats; eyes blanketed with boredom. It seemed to have been dusk since dawn and we suspected from the outset that the trip was a mistake. Our first instinct had been the one to trust: you never discover the same enchantment twice.

In my mind's eye I had pictured the place, as though we were expected, with a festive holly wreath fastened to the door, fairy lights, trugs spilling winter pansies and wild birds flocking for sunflower seeds. I had prepared my handshake with the agent, my nods to rival viewers. I could see them already clutching their brochures and masking their distrust with nervous smiles. But the little car-park was empty when we arrived, save for a red Ducati motorbike and there was no one waiting. The cottage itself had a broken, desolate air. The roses clawed at empty window-panes. Heaps of decaying leaves had collected on the step and it was clear that the property had been empty for some time.

Nonetheless we knocked, pressed noses to glass to glimpse the rooms within. Letitia had flown, taking with her the air of hospitality and fun which had so captivated us. Now, under a blank, unyielding sky, we were surprised to find that the hill bore down in an oppressive way. The towering scarp faced north, and, though it had not occurred to us before, we realised now that the houses under it must languish in shadow for several months of the year. Today this corner felt damp and remote, cut off as it was from the companionable village.

We would beat a retreat, warm up over a pint somewhere and take fresh stock of things, but this was easier said than done. As we turned to leave, an enormous Rhodesian Ridgeback shot out of the cottage next door and with a fearsome display of teeth, mounted guard at the garden gate. Hackles raised, ears flattened, she clearly saw us as intruders and had no intention of letting us pass. We 'townies', with a nervous distrust of every animal, promptly assumed that we were done for. But, to our relief, the owner, roused by the hullaballoo, now put in an appearance.

He was a young man, swarthy, muscular, clad only in a vest and jogging pants. Perhaps he had just got out of bed. His two-day beard and naked feet somehow suggested it. He pushed the hair out of his eyes and leaning against the doorpost, dispassionately took the measure of us.

"Oh drop it, Rosie," he drawled, after a while. The Ridgeback stopped and stared. "Come on girlie - don't make a pest of yourself!" He picked his way down the path and made a great show of hugging the beast and kissing it on the nose. "See? Daft as a baby, really." He smiled to reveal his own white teeth. "Just showing off. Were you coming to see *herself* next door? There's no one there. She's gone."

"We gathered that," Philip replied with a formal frostiness. He felt that some apology was owing.

"Funny business." Blackbeard straightened up, wiping his hands on his vest. So he had not been in bed, then. He had been doing a job - a dirty job of some kind - his hands were black. In a flash I remembered the motor-bike parked nearby and how, to the outrage of his wife, a friend of ours, who owned a Yamaha, used to clean his engine case in the dishwasher. When I took a closer look, I noticed that the air of dereliction affected both sides of the house -

a fact which had not dawned on me before. The dingy curtains on this side had been clumsily drawn. The end of a skip protruded into the garden. Yes, I decided, this man was exactly the sort who would wipe his dirty sprockets on a tea towel. The thought of that bike began to bother me. It had been so red, so shiny, aggressively asserting itself with its vermilion hellfire transfers.

"We were supposed to be meeting the agent," I explained.

"I wouldn't know about that," he gave his hands a final rub. "All I know is that the bird who lived next door here was a nutter. I'm almost glad she's gone."

"A *nutter?*" Well, he could hardly be expected to appreciate Kandinsky and anchovy tart. The refinements of a woman like Letitia must have been lost on him.

Having begun, however, he wanted to go on talking and since he and his dog both blocked the gate, we had no choice but to listen: "You wouldn't believe the goings on round here. Weird things. All to do with *her.*" He slid, for effect, into the present tense. "I haven't been here a week..." (so, he is a relative newcomer - that explains a lot) "...and *she* comes knocking me up at four o'clock in the morning. Four in the morning, I'm telling you. I think the place must be on fire. But no. She's got some garbled story about finding a man in her room. What she actually says to me is she's seen the Devil! Well, what am I supposed to make of that? Here I am, half naked, with this woman all but throwing herself at me." He was standing now, arms crossed, feet planted wide, thrusting his weight on his heels. "I'm not saying I'm beyond temptation, like, but she's a bit old for me. '*The Devil,*" she says, "*came up those stairs and stood at the foot of my bed.*' Near hysterical, she is. I make her a cup of tea and try to calm her down. She's having none of it. Me, I just want my sleep, so I let her ramble on. I suppose I'm too soft. Next week, she's back again. She's run out of milk and she's got some crazy story about seeing lights on the hill. Yeah, honest. After dark, she sees witches' covens dancing round those trees. I won't say we never had a bit of a fling. It seemed like fun at first. But she just spooked the hell out of me. She had psychopaths in the family, she said. I tell you what I did. I threw her out. I could see she was losing it.

10

She used to wander about up there in her nightie. And *candles*... I thought, with the thatch and the wooden beams and that, the whole bloody cottage was going to blazes."

Throughout this speech we had been edging along the path, looking for some possibility of escape. But Rosie had never taken her eyes off us and he was evidently enjoying himself. Having fastened on his subject, he had no intention of letting go and his menace of a smile was not to be trifled with. Foreign was he? No. His accent had a London twang. But there was something about him I could not place which made me feel we had stepped into unknown country.

"These cottages were one house once. The original stairs went straight up through the middle. I checked. The dividing wall is only wattle and daub, one layer thick - you can hear absolutely everything through that. When they put that in, the staircase had to go and they built new stairs at either end instead. Well, what do you think? At the dead of night, when I'm lying in my bed, I can hear footsteps creeping up and down those stairs. The stairs, I mean, that aren't stairs any more. They go straight to that woman's bedroom, next to mine. And then the power is always going off... I've had it with this place, I don't mind telling you. I'm out of here next week. I told her to knock it off or I would get the police. And guess what happens next? She only tops herself. Right there, in that study of hers. She was a blinking nutter all right. No mistake."

He looked at us with sudden hostility. "You friends of hers, or what, then?"

"Not at all," Philip, asserted himself. "We heard the place was up for sale and thought we would take a look, that's all. We're sorry to have bothered you."

"Well, I wish you luck of it." Perhaps his feet were getting cold. He gave a surly shrug and yanked his dog away. By the time he reached his own front door his expression had turned quite ugly.

"Don't believe me, do you? Well, go and look for yourselves. They're burying her today. I reckon I had a lucky escape. You want to watch out, too."

"If anyone's a nutter," said Philip, hustling me away, "it's surely *him*. A case of paranoia if ever I saw one."

11

I turned for one last look, hoping for a clue I might have overlooked. But man and dog had disappeared indoors and there was nothing to confirm my doubts. Was *he* the mysterious agent Letititia found whose contract brought her wealth and happiness? And had he come to claim her soul, once the money ran out? Had *she* made the fatal mistake of wanting too much... dreaming of what might lie on the other side, where chance blew like a cross-wind? Dreamers and outlaws... Cheating the Revenue - bribing Fate - paying blood money to appease the gods... And one could slip so easily from innocence into something deeper... The Hill was a dangerous place. I could see that now. The heart was a dangerous place, with windows opening onto the unknown. And all realities were essentially unreliable.

"You can see what has happened," said Philip, looking for cause and effect. "He's driven her out with his ravings and now he's using the same device to frighten prospective buyers. Could you imagine *her*, the woman we met in the summer, committing suicide, dying just like that? She was so full of life... Unless," a darker thought just crossed his mind, "unless he did her in."

The idea of being marooned with that fantasist, in such a lonely place, frankly appalled me. We had had a lucky escape. Nothing, I determined, would make me come within miles of the village again. My knees were actually shaking.

We left the car and headed into the village. The road curved past the church, half-eclipsed by yews in its sombre, green churchyard. For some reason my eyes were drawn to a spot on the northern side. A man in a donkey jacket was working there - piling the earth into a fresh-dug grave. Flowers lay heaped at his feet.

"Philip..." I began, but he marched me past.

"It's nothing to do with us," he said in a strange, peremptory way. I found myself propelled along the lane to the steps of The Fountain Inn. "We'll have a coffee and then get out of here."

Christmas greeted us at the door. Fresh greenery wreathed the rafters, aromatic, like the beer. A real log fire and fairy lights. The smell of oak soot. Home-made soup. Gin traps and antlers. It was warm and snug and sweet inside. A private function in an inner room kept the young waitress running back and forth with trays of sandwiches. The inn-keepers wife, demurely dressed in black, was polishing glasses with a distracted air.

"Are you with the party in *there?*" she inquired, nodding towards the door.

Philip shook his head. "Two coffees, please."

"Sit there in the window, lovie, and I'll bring them over. Friends of hers, were you?"

"Sorry?"

"Letitia. Were you friends?"

"We just came out for a drive." He had closed up like a scalded hand, all pleasantries dispensed with, but I could not help myself:

"You mean the woman who died?" I said. There was no need for rudeness.

"It's a bad business." The woman shook her head. "Whatever anyone says, she was a lovely girl. She used to come in here - buy anyone a drink. I never saw a person so generous with their money. Always cheerful. Always pleasant. Always interested. She had some funny friends I'll grant you - but you can't always choose your friends, now, can you? Especially in her particular line of work." She put her cloth on the counter and it seemed that she had said all she had to say. But soon she broke out again:

"There was no call for that nastiness over the grave."

"Nastiness?"

Philip gave me a kick of disapproval.

"Rector here. I must say he fancies himself. Always got a different coloured surplice on - you know the type. Flatly refuses to give her burial on the Christian side of the church. Just because they say she killed herself. They've got no proof. It could have been faulty wiring. And I wouldn't mind betting it was more than an accident. That fiend next door could have been up to something. He'd marked her out, you know. I reckon he bullied her." She leant across the bar, in confidence: "She was so successful. Some folks round here were just plain jealous. Said her books were rubbish. I don't know. I'm not the reading type. All I know is she was a worker, she kept at it, however hard it was. She did one of those correspondence courses. Became addicted, so she said. At first it went all right. She sold a couple of things and then just when she was in the flow, all the words dried up. She had this thing called writer's block. Couldn't put pen to paper. She liked to chat in here. Well, it's a lonely life, isn't it? Scribbling at home all day. She used to confide in me - she didn't mind who knew. There was no side on her at all. She was in debt, you know and things looked pretty bad. Then she did a deal with this new agent and it turned her life around. She found she could write again, only this time it was better. And money! She must have got herself a cracking advance. She bought that cottage down the lane outright. Had it all done up. Cash for everything! And the 'do's she had there before that man moved in... The London lot that came to visit her all rolled in here for drinks. It was our best season ever. Just one long party. And then, when it seemed things had never been so good, the horrible rumours began... and the scandals and now her dead." She looked up, surprised by tears. "I liked her."

Seeing her distress, I felt like a vulgar snooper. Whatever had possessed us to come? We had been peering through this woman's windows half the day, stumbling over her secrets, spying on her grave and now, when she had been stripped quite bare, a feast for carrion gossip, here we were, like rooks which had smelled dead meat, offended by our own rank appetites. We had been nothing but gate-crashers from the beginning - birds of ill omen, seeing things we had no right to see. We drank our coffee in silence and slipped away.

The day was clearing and a watery sun lacquered the flooded fields with sheets of light. High on the hill, the beeches still conferred, their trunks skewed by the prevailing wind. *We see on the other side...* A sap-starved sleep, dreaming of summer...

"I tell you what we'll do." Philip shook off his morbid mood, grabbed my hand and began to stride along. "We'll go back home and forget this ever happened. We don't *need* a cottage or an inglenook. We don't need promotion and a bigger car. We don't even need the lottery. I'm going to give that up. What we *do* need is cheese on toast... and a Christmas tree! Agreed?"

"Agreed," I answered, bravely swinging his arm. "You'd better let them know, though, all the same - that we don't want to view the cottage now, I mean. Ring them on your mobile. Then we are free."

The agent was out at lunch and our call was answered by a junior secretary.

"Mouse Cottage? Oh I'm terribly sorry," she said, swallowing the last of her sandwich. "That one is no longer available. The viewing this morning was cancelled."

"So it seems." She had rather taken the wind out of his sails. She was new to the job and eager to impress.

"We've got some others - really lovely ones." Perhaps she had been trained never to let the client end a call.

But Philip now felt aggrieved. "You might have let us know. We've had a wasted morning. And..." he searched for his words, "...one that was none too pleasant, as it happens."

"It was all so sudden," she babbled, in self-defence. "The buyer just came in and said she'd have it. Cash sale. No chain. No mortgage to arrange. She virtually put the money on the table. Loaded she was. Mr. Davies got on the phone to the owner and said *'for God's sake take the offer while she's keen'*. It was too good to refuse, he said, considering how hard the place had been to sell."

"A woman, you say?"

"That's right. A lady novelist. A bit of an Arty-fart, if you know what I mean, but terribly nice, even so. She said she'd had a stroke of luck." She paused. "I probably shouldn't be telling you all this."

"A *novelist*?" choked Philip. "Surely not *another*?"

"Sorry?" Perhaps the line was breaking up. Perhaps she thought we doubted her. Her tone became more defensive than before. "There haven't been any *others*. That's the *point*. No one would touch the place. It's been on the market, derelict, for years..."

Now I cannot say what Philip thought at that point, but for me the wind suddenly blew fresh from a new direction. If nothing we had seen was real in the conventional sense - mere shadows of possibility - projections, say, on the flimsy screen of the mind - then all was still to play for. Not just for us, but for Letitia too, Mouse Cottage, the whole of life. And perhaps we had misread the point about lotteries - the very secret the Five Brothers knew and

15

whispered on the wind. With Chance, everyone is *always* a winner. The numbers invariably come up. But the prizes, the prizes are different every time. On the darkest day of the year it was only natural that Old Nick should be in the ascendant. But another day? Another day we would be different people, seeing with different eyes and what lay on the other side would bring us equal surprise. And I knew as I scanned the long skyline that I would *have* to come back. I was not yet done with Rooks' Hill...

The Waiting Room

For Anyushka

The Waiting Room

Never having married, I do not know much about the raising of children, but as a dutiful great-uncle, I have come to learn a good deal about the lives of the young today. I note with approval the bright, airy spaces in which their infant minds develop. All is colour and light in their world. Their clothes are soft, their toys are clean. Their homes are safe from bugbears. Bed-time is a positive ritual of comfort and calm. They are plied with warm drinks and cosy stories, and friendly faces from nursery tales crowd round them on their walls. How could they but be happy, thus surrounded with loving care? My own beginnings were altogether less protected.

Not that I blame my parents in any way. They were of the most loving disposition. Indeed, they lavished upon us as much indulgence as was practically possible. They could not be blamed for cold sheets and draughty bathrooms; for the damp of mouldy corners and woodlice in cupboards. Such things simply *were* for many of my generation and if we endured them uncomplaining, with our hot-water bottles and knitted balaclava helmets, we later prided ourselves that hardship had forged our 'character' and made us strong. Nonetheless, I have to confess that my own childhood was, and for many years remained, a region of dread. To be sure, there were faces in every nook of the house, but they were such as imagination construed from random marks and cracks in the walls around me. Lions lurked in the marble patterns of the bathroom linoleum and stared, with knobs for eyes, from the dresser doors. A howling demon danced above my bed. Whole bestiaries lurked in the random folds of a curtain. One might say that for me face-making became a private compulsion. I certainly never spoke of the things I saw. They peopled the fringes of my consciousness, like the woodlice - afflictions to be borne in solitude. And to this day I can recall each particular squint or ghastly gape of mouth configured in the grain of a wooden door.

19

Was it something to do with living underground? Ours was a basement flat in a grey, Victorian terrace on the boundary between the towns of Brighton and Hove. In those days, before the two were joined together, they enjoyed separate identities - Brighton racy, bohemian, and Hove, all mothballs and lapdogs and though it was hard to see where the line between them lay, you knew as soon as you crossed it. Our terrace, Caroline Terrace, had its foot on this on this east-west boundary and commanded another threshold too, for from this point on, the towns' Regency elegance descended into a surf of redbrick and plaster. To the north, lay an expanse of Victorian suburbs, washed inland by the growing population. In effect, these farther districts formed a separate town, and as I grew up I would come to know that too. But to begin with there was just the basement. And the basement had a 'liminal' atmosphere.

I have only to think of it and my curious fingers trace the blisters on the painted, iron gate. My infant boot sinks into snow beside the wall. The house itself towers into terra incognita: a flight of crimson stairs mounting to unknown worlds above, and to either side more houses and grey streets which lead to a steel grey sea. I catch the roar of that now, caged behind railings, on which the paint has corroded, corrupted, erupted into deep-rusting sores. A maze of paving-slabs absorbs me, clinging, as I walk, to the warm safe-smelling folds of my mother's coat. Out there is danger - of that I have no doubt - a pitiless current into which one might be swept by a single, slate-backed wave. One glance at the houses bears out my conviction: to the front, all elegance - an iron fretwork of balconies and fanlight filigree; to the rear, a fearful jumble of that same metal, twisted into fire escapes - the menacing tackle of which has haunted my dreams for as long as I can remember.

Perhaps it was careless adult talk that dropped the seeds of fear into my mind. Gossip whispered by other children's parents when they were sure we were not listening. Bill-boards, telling of murders, of robberies, of fires in the great hotels, whose labyrinthine depths trapped victims half-asleep. Warnings of drowning, of dance halls where the drinks were spiked with dope. Hallucinations. And streets one never went to where the 'convicts' lived. I did not then know what a convict was. But I knew there was a black-walled church and in my mind the darkness and the fire-escapes and the stories of sudden death fermented into a strong, narcotic brew. I said that Caroline Terrace had a liminal air and certainly life there seemed to hang between rival worlds: the familiar here-and-now with its dressing-gowns and bedtime tales and buttered toast by the fire and then a shadow-side - a lawless region where anything at all might lie in wait.

What will today's infants remember? Is it true, as I suspect, that reason in time resolves our childish fears? Our cradle fantasies naturally change and mellow. Irrational doubts subside as time takes off at a gallop and our grown-up minds become too busy with plans to muse in idleness. I say this because such furniture as I still keep from those far-off days bears a different aspect now. I no longer see lion's eyes on the dresser doors, or hands on the rocking-chairs. Nowadays, I can view a hole in the ceiling without absolute dread. Normality, like logic, dulls the sense. But my family moved to a new house when I was seven and so my first impressions of many things retained their original vividness, cut off as they were from all that followed after. And since it is unsettling to remember the hold they had on me, they are mostly locked away, with other old, no-longer-needed things, in the lumber rooms and cellars of my mind. I can almost convince myself that they are gone. Only occasionally does something excite the intensity of feeling they once stirred in me. But just occasionally, something, tossed up like a sea pebble on the pavement beneath my feet, sends a shiver through the heart, a reminder that on the other side of all we know, lies an alien, foaming and fecund mass - the world of the Unseen. In such rare moments, I must confess the haunted sense returns that I am not alone - that some malevolent force is watching me.

Determined to avoid all links with the past, I decided, to move away and conduct my adult life in a distant place. I left my tumultuous schoolboy feuds at the red-bricked school on the hill, my grazed knees in the playgrounds, my aching feet at the bus stops and turned my back on the sea. I immersed myself in the optimism of Progress. Made money. Travelled. Laid down a cellar of wine. Insurance was my ticket to security, stability, an early pension even. How else could I have been the mainstay of my brothers and sisters and all their numerous children? How else, a model to all of how to succeed and prosper?

Notwithstanding all of which, every man has his weakness and mine is a morbid fear of dentists.

Frederick Duncton, BChD, FDSRCS, had his dental practice in one of the grander houses in Brunswick Town. Here the sea was green. A turbulent sky blazed above the Georgian façades. Gulls wheeled, crying in the wind. The walk there lay through the miniature wilderness of St. Anne's Well Gardens and my recollections of both dentist and garden became inextricably intertwined. There were crocuses in spring, spreading in pools beneath the trees, and leaves to scuff in autumn; dark bushes leading to a kiosk, where one could buy vanilla wafers, and the ruins of the well itself, a chalybeate spring which once attracted the cream of fashionable Brighton. Constable sat here to paint the wind whipping over the sea. But Constable was unknown to me then. The 'known' was a rising sense of dread. Each step led inexorably to the black and white steps, the brass doorplate, the deep-throated buzz of the bell... the dentist's waiting room. A sweet, antiseptic smell seemed to come from the walls and the walls were vast, papered in a timeless cream and grey-green pattern. There was a great, worn leather sofa, armchairs, a piano and a chandelier which intensified the gloom. A place built for giants, as I recall. The window reached almost from floor to ceiling. The doors were eight feet high. One wall consisted of a wooden screen, which must have opened on grand occasions, straight into the treatment room. From there one could hear the high-pitched whine of the dentist's drill and Frederick's laugh as he cracked another joke, for he was an immensely kind and jovial man. Time held its breath in that room. At the age of four, at ten, at sixteen, I knew just what to expect at Rothesay Place. Fillings were a fact of life. This I accepted unquestioningly. Fillings were as inevitable as school exams and falling over in the playground. Suffering without anaesthetic. But Frederick's methods, certainly old-fashioned by the 'seventies, held a theatrical fascination which somehow mitigated pain. The little Bunsen burner at which he sterilised his probes, the metal canister filled with plugs of cotton wool, the stands of drills, which, to my juvenile eye, looked like so many toy battleships; the ghastly wonder of the chair itself with its swivelling tables and lamps, its porcelain bowl and button-like dentist's stool - I noted all. Indeed, I would say no prisoner ever viewed the rack with more attentive interest. There were tweezers and swabs and pink stuff and grey stuff which seemed to be cooked in an oven and Frederick himself in his tight white jacket, looking for all the world like a corpulent chef, eyes twinkling as he boomed:

"Spit that out!"

"Have a rinse!" And blissfully:

"There. All done!"

Year after year, the ritual was the same. Life changed, life progressed. But the waiting room waited, as shadowy, as mysterious as ever. Here, as in the basement, were stairs which led to a world unknown. The window gave onto a treeless yard, its frosted glass blurring the outlines of the walls beyond with the cables of an antique service pulley, a relic from the days when this was a family house and had servants working below. By dint of association I grimly supposed the pulley to be some piece of dentist's equipment. And how was it that year after year, there were always workmen digging up the road? The place shuddered perpetually to the roar of pneumatic drills.

In time, I took a more impartial view; listened for echoes from the silent walls and, in my mind, swung back the folding doors to disclose the original ballroom, set for a dance. There would have been candles here. And mirrors. And footmen. Carriages at the door. The trick worked wonders and I would be in the dentist's chair before there was time thumb a magazine.

The odd lapse was unavoidable. Once, on a November afternoon, I arrived as dusk was falling. The bell, usually answered by Frederick's wife, triggered some new, automatic device and the door mysteriously opened on its own. The hall was dark, but a strip of light from the surgery, suggested Duncton was there. Shutting the door behind me, I tiptoed along the passage and sat in the waiting room. A deathly hush lay over the place. No burst of good-humour from the room next door. I must have been a young lad then, on the cusp of adolescence - thirteen perhaps - old enough to travel unescorted and yet too shy to turn the light on for myself. A late, crepuscular blue glimmered at the window. The furniture crouched in a shadowy mass. It was cold. Ice cold. I remember thinking that a braver person would have lit the gas in the antique, black-singed heater which filled the hearth. I knew from years of study just where it stood. That over there was the piano, that the armchair with the button missing... that the low table with its copies of *Private Eye*. Feelings of desolation gradually stole over me. As the darkness intensified, however, my eyes adjusted to the change and soon I found I could see things better than before. To my surprise I made out the figure of a man, whom I had not noticed before, on the shabby chesterfield. He must have waited so long he had actually gone to sleep. His head lolled back at an alarming angle. And he was dreaming, for his eyelids moved from time to time, lifting to reveal an upturned strip of white. I had seen my mother do this when she was ill and it filled me then with a peculiar horror. This man was elderly, dressed in a gabardine. His pale hand held a stick - fingers like white roots, I thought - cross-veined. They seemed to have grown in that position, bringing to mind the embrace of a strangler-fig. Bald head, skin stretched tight across the temples. His shoes... His shoes were dusty, long and very thin. An ordinary sight and yet, in that unnatural gloom, an apparition so appalling that I finally roused myself. By a conscious and convulsive effort I forced my attention onto something else. My mind dilated upon the dividing screen, willing the jointed panels to yield and part. In poured a stream of dancers. Epaulettes and powdered wigs. Pumps. Diamonds. Ringlets. Laughter. *Anything* imagination could conjure up for human company. Moments later the vision vanished under an electric glare and there stood Mrs Duncton at the door, fussing apologies:

"So sorry! *So* sorry! We had an emergency. I should have left a light. We had a sudden emergency at home. The dog got its head stuck in a gate. Of course we *had* to go. What a disaster! But everything turned out all right in the end. The fire brigade were wonderful. *Thank* you for waiting. He'll see you in a moment or two. I hope you weren't afraid sitting all alone in the dark!"

I mention this episode for its being the very last time I yielded to morbid fantasy.

When Frederick retired, a young chap took his place. I tried another dentist nearer home, but that cheery practice proved too much of a change for me. The strategies I had developed to quell my nerves proved ineffectual here. At this new clinic there was nowhere to hide. Under a blaze of surgical white, the array of drastic and exorbitant treatments and the amalgam of music and perfect smiles frankly appalled me. Anxious for my purse *and* my crooked teeth, I scuttled back to Hove and registered once more at Rothesay Place.

Here were the familiar steps; the polished plate of yore; the husky bell; the high hall and the waiting room, refurbished with flowers and drapes. All was new - yet the bones of the old remained. Here I could .reach across the years to myself, the timid child. Memories of old terrors raised a patronising smile. How absurd to be afraid of a staircase or an empty chair. How ridiculous, hearing voices in the chimney! What a relief to have left that haunted world behind.

On my last visit there I was accompanied by my great-nephew, Thomas. A boarder at a country preparatory school, he was one of those children whose life had been lived entirely in a cocoon of colour and light. Since his grandparents spent most of their time in in Scotland and his parents worked abroad, I had visited him often at his school and seen for myself the delightful setting, the homely atmosphere, the bright and modern furnishings and the genial informality he and his classmates enjoyed - so different from the austerities of the past. Gone were the stone floors, blackboards and pink blancmange of my old school days. Carpets! Computers. Hallowe'en parties... Thomas was thirteen, the oldest boy in his class and soon to graduate to the main school in Brighton. Alec and Fran being held up in Karachi, and the in-laws off on a retirement cruise, I volunteered to take the boy along for his interview. It was the end of Autumn Term, and we had crammed the car to the roof with Thomas's gear - I could hardly credit how

25

much stuff he had. Our goodbyes said, the house-mistress waved us off, and we motored down to Brighton for our lunch. There were ten young pupils trying for a place, but Tom was the only one to apply as a music scholar. He took it all in his stride; embracing the chance to show what he could do. Not that he was a bragger. But he had a confidence, and easy balance of mind, which I must confess I envied, despite my years. He tucked into his pizza with absolute equanimity. And when I mentioned my own appointment and asked if he minded waiting while the dentist drilled me, he nodded in a cheerfully abstract fashion. It was all the same to him. He had never had a filling.

Once more, I was reduced to wonder at the advances which have been made in the raising the young. Soon, I predicted, we could live in a world where there were no neurotics, no neurasthenics, no taint in society of paranoid disturbance. A sunshine world of reason beckoned this generation forward. What need would they have for the torments I had known? I daresay Thomas had never had a nightmare. One might as well ask if he sucked his thumb as intimate that the dark was dangerous. Both would have been an insult. Neither could have made any sense to a boy with his disposition.

The scholarship interview passed off agreeably. My nephew, being a dab hand at sums, breezed through his entrance paper. All that remained was an audition for the choir, but here he encountered a setback, for something peculiar began to affect his voice. At first we thought he was going down with a cold. Whenever he tried to speak he growled, then squeaked, surprising himself, like a young cockerel learning to crow.

The music master laughed. "It's that age, I'm afraid! Always happens when it's least convenient. Usually the voice breaks just before a concert - pardon?" He was recovering from a cold himself and finding it hard to hear, so he was delighted the audition must be postponed.

That age... just on the cusp of adolescence - not a child, not a man - a half-thing in a world made suddenly strange. I felt a secret pride and tenderness when I looked at him. He had *made* it - arrived, so to speak, on the hither shore, blissfully unaware of the perils travelled through. Now Christmas was upon us. Alec and Fran would be back in a couple of days. Lila was coming home from her French exchange. The whole family would be together, safe and sound.

Rothesay Place looked resplendent in the afterglow of a setting winter sun. Promotion to city status had done much for this town and the seafront streets and squares had shaken off their former dinginess in a frenzy of paint and potted cordylines. The basements now were all designer chic and treated passers-by to tasteful glimpses of white walls and Swedish pine. Here we were already at number ten and the old brass bell was looking as shiny as ever.

We were shown to the waiting room by a smiling nurse. No need for the gas fire now. The place was filled with ambient warmth and the chandelier had gone. Instead, a contemporary fitting lit the room with a bright and comforting light. As luck would have it, we had the place to ourselves. I sat, as was my custom, facing the window and the sky beyond, now deepening into dusk. Thomas, oblivious to all around him, got out his mobile phone and began to amuse himself with a game of Hangman. How different everything seemed. The piano, the pulley, the pneumatic drills - *long gone* - appeared to my mind as incongruous now as though they had never been. When my turn came, I gave my boy a nod.

"I won't be long. You'll be all right here, won't you?"

He barely acknowledged my words - merely gave me a wave with his unoccupied hand, his gaze fixed steadfastly upon his screen.

Twenty minutes later I collected him. We emerged into lamplight and walked the length of the street. As we did so, a sense of euphoria came over me. We had survived. How many times had I felt that in this place? Duty accomplished, I was a boy again. Our trials over, we were free to enjoy all the pleasures of Christmas coming, and satisfaction in what we had achieved. My great-nephew, Thomas! What an inspiration he was!

As we reached the car, he put his phone away and turned to face me with a curious look. I was blithely unprepared for what came next:

"Did you see that man in the waiting room?" he said, mouthing the words, as though he was half afraid someone might overhear. Then he gave what I can only describe as a shudder.

"HE NEVER ONCE TOOK HIS EYES OFF YOU!"

Foul Deeds

For Muriel

Foul Deeds

'No one stayed long at The Rectory, Upper Sniping. Some houses accumulate an atmosphere over time. Some are built at sites already known for qualities hard to define: a thickening of the air; an unearthly resonance, or timbre. One may call these phenomena, (which manifest themselves from time to time to the sensitive among us), psychic influences, or ghostly vibrations or pure imagination and poppycock. The fact remains: no one stayed long at The Rectory.

'The house, a stone affair, with large sash windows and a gabled roof, surmounted by owl-shaped finials, reposed amongst trees on a hill above Romney Marsh. At the crown of the hill stood the new church, for the old, a remnant, two miles distant on the flatlands below, had been abandoned, along with its plague-ridden village, Sniping Eldre, in the 14th Century. This Saxon structure, having been used as a barn by generations of farmers, was now a mere stump, the roof having fallen in. That the new church dated from 1350 and so was not new at all, made no difference to its name. And that the house beside it - once home to a servant of St. Augustine's Priory, Canterbury - was stripped of its occupant during the Dissolution and, together with the Archishop's Palace, given into secular hands, made no difference either, for the place clearly belonged with the church and was soon reclaimed by the Crown, (the owner having lost his place at court over some minor misdemeanour) and restored to a clerical incumbent. It was not long, therefore, before ecclesiastical footsteps and the rustle of vestments were once more heard on the flagstones. A hysterical servant girl noted them at dead of night, long after her master was abed, and swore in the morning that she had met a ghost. In truth, it was widely held that spirits from the past might rise with the marshland fogs and revisit to their former homes. And though the new protestant minister railed against such tittle-tattle and insisted, he being a rationalist, that since the dead were Catholic

31

and the Catholics had been banned by Royal Decree, they could not meddle with living Christian souls, he nonetheless found it more commodious to move his family to a house on the Hartshorn road and ride to church on horseback. The worthy folk of Sniping, thus relieved of a moralist in their midst, continued a lively trade in contraband wool and preserved such pagan beliefs as kept them well-furnished with fireside tales. That was before the Civil War and the Royalist uprising in which The Marsh took little part, though consequences sometimes trickled through. One day, Cromwell's men brought Sniping a puritan pastor - a regular Leveller, dressed in a capotain hat, and lately come from Northamptonshire. Coverfew was his name, which made the locals laugh, since he had no sooner arrived than his dwelling burnt to the ground and every simpleton knew that, in a wooden house, it was wise to cover one's fires at night with a curfew or 'couvre feu'. This firebrand, nothing daunted, got up in the pulpit and exhorted all men to return to an honest life. To their further discomfiture he declared that he must live amongst his flock and promptly established himself in the original Rectory. "Simplicity. Humility, brothers. A new beginning." He planted beans, berated adulterers and purged the village alehouse of its ale. As soon as was feasible, he was himself thrown out and the ne'er-do-wells of Sniping drank the new King's health and re-lit their smugglers' lamps.'

Jennifer Armitage took off her glasses and pressed her fingers into her eyes. How exhausting it was to read small print on a screen! But the Records Office staff were strict about it. Digital viewing only of the rarest documents. Deacon Bradley's *'Survey of the Unhallowed Houses of Kent'* had been a private publication - a mere sixty copies, from a local hand-press, distributed to his friends. At least forty-five had been destroyed by a fanatic, so it was a miracle that the text survived at all. Strain or no strain, she felt she *must* struggle through it.

She was not a suggestible woman. She worked for a building society. She had a husband and son and life was going well. Only two months ago they had moved to a house in a brand new village development - left the noise and congestion of Maidstone and seized the chance to follow their dream of a life in the countryside. The house at Rectory Court gave them a pristine slate: white walls, shiny, laminate floors, soft-closing kitchen units. a barbeque area and a *view* - the famous Sniping vista across the Marsh. When she first set foot in the hall she felt a shiver of excitement. The place had a 'lived-in' feel - an ambience all its own. What better welcome could the family hope for? There was a village bus to get young John to school, and a superstore where she could pick up supper after a long day at her desk. Certainly there were the usual teething problems: the internet didn't work and the fuse box seemed to have a mind of its own, the switches tripping for the silliest reasons. But on the whole, they congratulated themselves on the best move of their lives.

Soon afterwards, Jennifer suffered the first of her 'turns'. She had come home early to meet a man who was going to fix the shower - unaccountably, the fitting had come apart and was lifting away from the wall. *"Shoddy workmen! Cowboys! I'll get you sorted out."* He sounded friendly enough - trustworthy too. As she let herself in through the door, she heard water running.

"Andrew, is that you?"

Could it be that her husband, wanting to help, had arrived ahead of her? Or had the plumber decided to start the job on his own? No, that was impossible. Her head began to reel. Had the pressure pump sprung a leak or worse? A flood? Something met her at the foot of the stairs and blocked her way. A thickness. A nausea. She panicked, crying out:

"Is anyone there?" And then she realized that the sound was not water at all but the sound of a tree - a massive lime tree, rustling in the wind. The whole business lasted a moment, no more, and when she recovered her wits she remembered there *was* no such tree. She had had a fit of giddiness - lost her head. Perhaps it was a flash migraine. She needed a cup of tea.

After that, she found herself lingering longer in the supermarket aisles. As the winter nights drew in, the problem of choosing a bottle of wine could detain her so long the security manager made a note of her. John would be back by five but Andrew rarely made it home before seven o'clock. His job was in the City.

33

On days when John played football after school, she would dally interminably over the shopping, drive home and park the car and then, still seated at the wheel, begin to check her emails or a make a series of calls on her mobile phone, *anything* to postpone going in alone, for there had been other times when she did not feel safe indoors. Reassured by the sound of her son's approach, she would rouse herself and find her key as though she had just arrived. But her behaviour smacked of neurosis and she knew it. Friends, to whom she confessed the matter, suggested overwork. Perhaps it was depression. Had she thought of doing pilates? Had she spoken to her doctor? High blood pressure could cause the strangest symptoms. Her mother thought it was probably her age.

In all other respects the move was a great success. There were rambles on the hill behind the village for she and Andrew were enthusiastic walkers. There were sociable summer evenings with fairy lights and prosecco and women's chat around the chimenea, while the men drifted indoors to check their football. Everyone loved the house. Everyone envied the built-in storage cupboards. the luxury bathrooms - not one, but *two* of them, naturally. Christmas had been a dream. The non-stick rotary roaster produced the perfect turkey. The newly ordered sofa came in time and after dinner they all put on their slipper-socks and slumped together, watching films by electric candlelight. New Year brought promotion and a break in the Pyrenees. And when John won a place at a sports academy, Jennifer felt her cup was running over.

As long as voices filled the air, the house met all her fondest expectations. She simply could not explain her sense of dread when the place was empty. She almost felt ashamed to mention it. Once John began his course at Paddock Wood he was hardly ever at home. She got into the habit, doubtless regrettable, of stopping after work at 'The Pack Horse Inn' and spending an hour or two there with a book. The place had been made to look like a coffee bar and if she ignored the drinkers by the door, she could sip a leisurely cappuccino and persuade herself she deserved a chance to unwind.

Naturally, it did not take long for her to attract attention, but she did not want to talk to anyone here. She wanted to dissolve into anonymity. She wanted time to think. *She could not face the house.* She had come to believe, incredible as it seemed, that some unearthly thing had taken up residence there. If she was upstairs, 'the thing' was downstairs. If she went down, it moved into the kitchen or slipped past her and took refuge on the landing. On one occasion she persuaded herself that it was in the cupboard under the stairs. She stood, staring transfixed at the handle of the door. She knew she must open it - that if she did not, 'the thing', whatever it was, would have won. She must keep it on the move, but a helpless terror paralysed every limb. Finally, she wrenched the cupboard open. Of course there was nothing there, yet the prickling, tormented feelings continued, keen as ever.

After the prickling, came knockings and creakings…

Andrew laughed at her. "It's a new house, silly. It's got to settle in. The wood was green. Now it's seasoning. Everything moves in a new house. Why else do you think we've got a crack in the bathroom wall?"

It was true. There were hair-line cracks appearing all over the place. The window catches didn't meet properly. Hinges complained. Andrew, ever vigilant, with his oil can and plaster-filler, put it all to rights. Three weeks later she'd find another crack.

She began to keep her fears to herself, believing she was going off her head. Then one day at the pub, old Peter Milden sat himself down at her table and hooked a finger over the spine of the book she was reading.

"You aren't the first you know," he said curling his 'r's like a proper Romney man.

"I'm sorry?"

"You aren't the first to come in 'ere like this. There were others afore you from The Old Rectory."

She shrank back instantly, snatching her book away. The man peered on with unwelcome familiarity, his pink-rimmed eyes loose in their sockets, heavy jowls streaked with red as though he had been out in the wind.

The houses in Rectory Gate, she knew, occupied the site of an older property. The original gate had been saved and built into a

35

wall. But it had somehow never occurred to her to ask who had lived on the spot before.

"Last woman", Peter Milden confided, "she were a plannen consultant. Some big job, she 'ad, up Ashford way. She tried everythen but she couldn't stay in that place alone, no more'n you."

Disgusted at being approached by this reprobate, she felt a sudden conflict of desire. She did not want to be seen talking to him, but what he said roused her curiosity. Perhaps there was something he knew - perhaps something all the secretive hearts of Sniping knew, which she, too, ought to know. Perhaps she was not going mad.

"Tell me," she heard herself say. "Why was the Old Rectory demolished?"

"It weren't exactly demolished," he leaned closer, breathing out the stink of his beer. "Kind of demolished itself."

"Tell me!"

He put down his empty glass and rubbed his nose with his finger, then blew out a sigh as though she were asking too much.

"I'll buy you a pint," she offered.

And he rubbed his nose again and smiled, disclosing a row of tombstone teeth. "Bitter," he said, now rubbing his hands on his thighs: "Very kind I'm sure."

When she returned to the table, he had spread himself at his ease.

"Where to start?" he mused. "S'pose I go backwards. This woman from London - Mrs. Struthers, they called her - she used to drink in 'ere. She done the whole place up. Ripped out walls, put in winders. The money she spent on that place wasn't nobody's business. She put a few noses out of joint on the parish council, I can tell you. Everyone thought she was after the money, like. Of course, she'd got all the right connections with her work. There were skips out in the street month after month and the guts of the house, they all come out in pieces. The kitchen units what the previous people had. Baths. Wardrobes. All of it practically noo an' only just put in."

"And did she sell on?"

"Couldn't, could she, after the place was condemned?"

"Why, whatever happened?"

"Sommat someone else had done, when they dug the damp course ditch."

"Was it subsiding?"

"Built on runnen sand, they said. It's a funny stuff. Once it starts falling in there's nowt you can do."

"My house is full of cracks."

"There y'are then." Old Peter smacked his lips.

"But that doesn't explain why the woman was afraid."

"Did I say that? Ah, well perhaps you're right. To make sense of it you'd have to go further back. All I know is she told me there was something not right with the place. She reckoned it was *haunted*."

"And was it?"

He shrugged, dipped his finger in a puddle of beer and began doodling patterns on the table. His next words came out slowly, timed and weighted for dramatic effect.

"So-o my grandmother said. She were house-keeper there afore they laid the electric on. The fires used to go out in the parlour for no reason. The place was always full of smoke. And she was always sure she could hear footsteps on the path behind the kitchen. Only there weren't no path by the wall there then, you see? She didn't like the back bedroom, neither."

"What happened?"

"She married and moved further down into the village. But that's the room where the old lady who lived there died. She was a psychic."

"Psychic?"

He nodded: "Queer old bird. They always said she must have frightened herself to death."

"That's gossip and rubbish, isn't it?"

"*You* hear anything?"

Suddenly she wanted to get away. "Nothing at all. I don't believe in ghosts."

"What you doin' in 'ere then, every night?"

"We're saving electricity." She grabbed her bag and fled.

37

Such information, disturbing as it was, came as a straw for drowning hope clutch at. If the old house, the one whose footprint maybe lay beneath her own, had been haunted, well then it stood to reason that some spirit might linger on. If a ghost could walk through a wall, would it even notice when the wall was no longer there? She needed to see the deeds. A ghost might be laid to rest. The Church could see to that. It should be easier to cure than a mind deranged. From that day forward she was too busy to sit in bars or coffee shops. Emboldened, she embarked on a quest, a wild pursuit of clues which led her into deeper, darker corners.

Her husband thought she was having an affair. And in a sense she was, though not an affair of the heart. Night after night, *he* ate a solitary supper while *she* attended meetings of the local History Group or pored over papers at the Record Office, where the relevant deeds had been deposited. The fat, vellum bundles, in indecipherable script, gave dates and names which she checked in the parish registers. From there it was but a step to the census returns, the graveyard plans of tombs. She was lifting lids, peeping into the lives, into the very coffins of the departed. The planning archives yielded further treasures, with details of building works: the wash-house demolition, attic conversion, the garage and flat-roof extension. Every attempt to clear the past, and let in light and logic, merely compounded the muddle of the house. The chimneys wouldn't draw, the windows wouldn't close. The finest insulation could not help when the boiler was on the blink. And no one ever understood why the pilot light went out as soon as the engineer departed.

Jennifer's files on the Old Rectory grew. And she uncovered more surprises. For instance, the list of rectors at Upper Sniping was particularly long. Ministers seemed to last a year or two at most. One could put it down to the damp from the marsh, or the winter winds, whipping up the Channel, but there was more to it than that. Some met with accidents. One was actually murdered. Several died young or begged to be moved to a more congenial spot. As for their families, the details stretched into endless elaborations.

"Of course," said Linda Prickett, her mentor, so to speak, at the local library, "you could always try and get hold of Bradley's book. Mind you, it's not strictly history - more gossip and fairy tales - but I believe Sniping gets a mention in it. The most interesting thing about that book was its suppression. Somebody claimed that it inspired all the other tales of hauntings on the Marsh."

Jennifer made note. Her research was taking on a dynamic existence of its own. It had already changed her life and the lives of those around her. But she could not say that it brought her any closer to 'the thing' she had confronted in the house. If anything, 'the thing' seemed to be in retreat.

"That's what you want, isn't it?" said her therapist. "Exorcism by force of Reason. You'll see."

Jennifer was not so sure. She wanted more. She wanted a tangible cause - something large enough, deep enough to have cut through the intervening clutter of the years. Mere 'thingness' was not enough. Perhaps Bradley could help.

She had skipped through the introductory notes - the tolling of church bells heard on autumn nights from ruins on the fog-bound flats below. Riders who vanished through walls and horses found half dead in their stalls after stormy nights. Such stuff was the stock-in-trade of smuggling men. And for centuries the Marsh had held almost more smugglers than sheep.

The unhallowed houses of Kent were ten a penny, according to Bradley, and his writing, with its endless dependent clauses, took some getting through. But he was Jennifer's last hope. She screwed up her eyes, put her glasses back on her nose, and applied herself once more:

'...certainly the Reverend Ozias Clarke,' the text continued, 'being suspected of helping the smugglers' cause and storing contraband tea in a hole in his pulpit, not to mention sending signals from the steeple when the Excise were abroad, was a probable candidate for any of the ghosts which infested the Rectory. And if, as is claimed, his successor, Robert Abel, sheltered a starving woman in his house and thereafter preached 'Bread or Burning' sermons to the Squire; if, as I say, it is true *that this woman bore his child and that, she dying in childbirth in his second best bed, and the child being unaccounted for, he slipped out of the parish, before the law, hot on his heels, could capture him, well, the likelihood is that he left some trace behind, like many another friend of Captain Swing who did or did not get a noose round his neck...*

Did every place resonate with similar stories?

By 1850 there was Daniel Small - a hawk-like man who contrived to drown in a well and in 1862 John Drayburn, the occultist. His collection of books was said to fill two floors and visitors testified that his library made noises in the night. The shadows of birds flew through the air when he opened certain pages. And the verger, passing his windows after dark, swore he heard dreadful cries within, like a cat caught in a fire.

Splendid as such tales were, they did not help. They were the stuff of legend, along with the grey ladies and wailing infants of every ancient building in the country, but they did not match the disturbances in the Armitage house.

Bradley published his book in 1868, two years after the Reverend Drayburn was found, stifled by smoke in his drawing room, but Drayburn's successor raised a violent objection to it. Tourists began to arrive at The Old Rectory. Seekers after thrills. To him it was no laughing matter. No matter for speculation either. He himself began to buy and burn the books. It seemed the strain of it all had turned his brain. He began to burn not only books, but pictures too, clothes and furniture. Night after night the bonfires could be seen from the steps of the vestry porch, with the Rector, in his night-shirt, running round them. On hearing this, the church authorities intervened. A replacement minister was sent and a local benefactor offered a different house; a house less damp, less dark, and definitely not so prone to infestations of brown flies up the chimney. From that day forth, this New Rectory provided for the ministers of Sniping.

As for the Old, it was swept and cleansed. New windows, new stairs, new wallpapered partitions transformed it into a model Victorian villa. They put in water pipes, a cooking range and a cheerful nursery. In turn these were followed by gaslight, baths, electricity, dado rails, Artex and central heating. Last, but not least, came the modern makeovers: paint stripping; wall stripping; doors, walls, fireplaces, rafters exposed, one after the other, till the house stood stripped to its naked bones, and still, it seemed, the residents would not stay. At last, when no more could be done to oust the cobwebs of the past, Jean Struthers, the planning consultant, gave up and left, and the property stagnated on the market. By stealth, the process of decay which had defined its history, returned and carried on its lethal work.

"It was a scandal!" Linda Prickett said. "It should have been listed. *Such* an important place. The whole business was a stitch up from the first. I don't mean to offend you, because I know you bought your place in good faith, and how could you know what you were paying for? But the developer put in a bid two weeks - *two weeks* before the subsidence cracks appeared. You're not going to tell me they had nothing to do with it! It was a stitch up. I don't believe it couldn't have been fixed. And now all we have left is a wall with a sand-blasted owl stuck on top!"

"I don't think the history is the point," Jennifer heard herself reply.

"I saw it myself." The other had wound herself up and now she was running, nothing was going to stop her. "In the morning it was standing. One afternoon was all it took. By tea-time it was just a heap of rubble. I daresay they saved some bits and pieces, though by all accounts there was precious little left. But it shouldn't have been allowed to happen. It's the principle of the thing."

Jennifer responded to the word.

"No, 'the thing' was something else," her voice sounded quiet but sure.

"I beg your pardon?"

"I looked into it all. When they dug our footings they carried out an archaeological search. There was nothing whatsoever in the ground. Not even a ring or a silver stater. The more I have learnt the less I have been able to see. I can stand in my hallway now and feel NOTHING."

"So?"

41

"So my husband says *he* wants to move. The place is giving him the creeps. It won't stay still."

Linda Prickett stopped and stared at her.

"And the fact is," Jennifer added, "that I suddenly feel depressed. Not just depressed but jealous too. It was *my* ghost and it seems to have abandoned me. I can open the windows on a windy night and gaze at the space where the old lime tree once stood and *there is nothing there*. I can put out all the lights and hold my breath till my heart is ready to burst. *Nothing*. It picks on you when you're not looking. It is something so ancient no house can ever hold it. It didn't ever want to BE in a house! And I see that Andrew and I have been a great nuisance to it. We wanted sole occupancy. Our names only on the deeds. But at the end of the day deeds are neither here nor there. We had no idea what our contract really meant."

She heard her voice running on, like the voice of a stranger and at this point, Linda Prickett knew that something was wrong:

"Don't you see? 'The Thing' didn't want to be with us at all. It will slowly destroy our house, as it did the house before, in the hopes of being alone. And do you know what? I wish in some way we could all stop being so busy and let it."

Beyond the Black River

Beyond the Black River

From his earliest years, Piers Farnaby had the look of a stalker. A pale, reclusive child, he made few friends at school and would take the daily journey home alone, dodging the taunts of bigger boys and sneaking through the sidecuts and alleyways of his native town, his satchel bumping against his legs, his head full of nonsense, cap dirtied from the latest playground scuffles. Mother would make it all right. Mother smoothed his hair and gave him Marmite for tea and said he would show them all when he grew up. And grow up he did. But he retained a fondness for lonely places and secrets. Secrets gave one power above the common advantages of strength or beauty. Other boys kissed pretty girls; other boys scored goals at football. Piers had no hope of competing in these matters, but he knew things which they would never know. He made it his business to know. And the knowledge sat within him, firm as a bank deposit against the day when it might be needed. Though the living seemed blind to his personal merits, there were others besides the living, he felt sure. And it did not take his imagination long to furnish forth characters from the past to people his world. These companions were his and his alone. They could not be corrupted by classroom gossip. They did not have to be placated with tribute money in the form of penny chews or marbles and they formed a flank of potent allies in his daily battle for survival. Through them Piers pursued his interest in shady places and the backstreet run to his house evolved into something uniquely pleasurable - an encounter with an 'other' world in which none but he believed.

The noses of some connoisseurs are so refined they can detect the year of vintage, nay, the very hillside where grapes have ripened, merely by sniffing a glass of wine. Piers developed a palate for atmosphere. Some places he dismissed as 'thin', quite lacking in body or 'bouquet'. But others had collected substance, as corners collect cobwebs, and Brighton abounded in such corners in the days when Piers was young. There were abandoned houses, boarded-up houses, neglected gardens a-plenty. There were peeling walls and dim basements and chequerboard steps of broken marble where pale weeds grew. Tenements eaten away by the salt, sea air. Yards full of junk. Dilapidated shops and old, high offices reverberating still to a racket of typewriters. Here he loitered and pried, feeding his taste for gothic fantasy and longing for a glimpse, or a ghostly shiver of something which would confirm his sense of belonging.

Heaven knows, he might have been murdered, peeking in at broken windows as the dusk was falling. And many a time he frightened himself with his thrilling suppositions. But nothing resembling a visitation ever revealed itself to him. An ordinary person at this point, would have lost interest and turned to something else. But Piers did not care for the things other lonely children liked. He wanted validation. And he meant to find it.

Long afterwards, the steward at the Brighton Museum would remember the pale-faced lad who hung about the collection of a Saturday morning. There he would be, ghosting between the cabinets of stuffed birds and mandolins, hovering over the flint axe heads and shards of Samanid-ware, his figure refracted in the glass till sometimes there seemed a dozen boys in gabardines and gartered socks, all pulling away at their lower lip, brows furrowed in concentration. He used to worry about that boy. Was he out to pinch something? Didn't he have a home to go to?

The steward would close his eyes for forty winks and glance up to find the gallery empty. Piers had moved on to look at curios in The Lanes, for if anywhere offered inspiration for a quaint imagination, 'The Lanes' was the perfect place. A tumble of roofs and narrow walkways, dog-legging this way and that between converging walls. Hidden gardens. Gateways to obscurity. A bustle of old book-lovers and gypsy women selling heather and rough types bundling in and out of smoke-filled pubs. Hippies arrived in the '70s, bringing noisy boutiques which spilled out onto the pavements with racks of Indian scarves and the reek of patchouli. When Council rates went up, many old shops moved out and high class shoes and chocolates moved in, but before the new world of the internet scooped their trade, the original folk of The Lanes were the dealers: stamps, coins, books, antiques... Did you need a halberd or a Samurai sword? An Amazonian butterfly? A first edition? This was the place to come, for here, with the screech of seagulls overhead, lay the dreaming heart of the town. What need for a museum, when every shop window was crammed with history, the more obscure the better? Piers began to collect.

At first his purchases were small: battered copies of the classics from the outside shelves of second-hand bookshops. The assistants viewed him with distrust, suspecting some pilfering, but he was always scrupulously honest. He handed over his pocket money and bore his treasures home, stowing them in folded paper bags at the back of his bedroom cupboard, lest his mother, ignorant of their value, should find them and put them in the rubbish bin. From books he made the transition to postcards, train timetables and other affordable junk. But the things he loved the most lay in the dim interior of Digby and Dawkins, half-way down Meeting House Lane. Digby and Dawkins specialized in sets of chess. Chess sets from Persia and chess sets from India. Some made of ivory, some of crystal, some of baked Sumerian clay. There were dumpy pawns carved from whales' teeth and walrus tusk and medieval knights rigged out for a joust. The whole history of mankind stood ranked in those battle lines. From the modernist, abstract forms of the Muslim pieces, to jade fantasies from China, Norman castles, French bishops, Sumatran monkeys... they were all equally beyond his means. But to hold the pieces in one's hand, to place them, as hands had placed them centuries before, make them live, dance, die, that would confer almost godlike power - a possibility Piers found irresistible. Never having the courage to enter the shop, he set about learning all he could by other means. Charles Brandrith, who sold military medals two doors down, was well informed and happy to gossip and Piers bought fistfuls of buttons and tarnished badges for the chance to hear him talk. Digby, he learned, was no longer an active partner, having passed away a number of years before and his survivor, Dawkins, was an acerbic chap. At one time he had been a cheerful neighbour, but of late he had given up being sociable and took a defensive line, as though he expected some unpleasantness. *Knowledgeable though,* nodded Brandrith. *He had been for many years a leading member of the Brighton Antiquarian Society - knew all about the early excavations on the Downs. He had written monographs, read the occasional paper up in London too. Now he kept his shop door locked, to the fury of the Americans, who wanted to come in and buy.*

Piers used to spy on him as he pottered behind his counter.

Years passed and the pale-faced schoolboy grew into a hollow-chested youth. The same straw-coloured hair, the same turbid eye made him instantly recognizable, but he did not fulfil his mother's expectations. While other boys went away to college, he took a job as a filing clerk at one of the bigger banks and spent his solitary lunch-hours retracing the paths he knew. Why should he care if the world had overlooked him? There was always chess. He cut out the daily puzzles from the newspapers. Saved his wages. Mugged up on the history of the game. Studied strategy... If he was timid in life, he would be ruthless on the board. He whiled away his evenings preparing himself. One day, he still believed, he would startle the world. And Dawkins' door, once locked, would be thrown wide to admit him.

But Fate has a way of wrecking our finest plans. Just when he had amassed enough money to buy a set of his own, the dusty chess shop in The Lanes unexpectedly closed. He remembered it exactly for it happened on New Year's Eve. A card on the door the following day read: "*Due to unforeseen circumstances...*" As ill luck would have it, it seemed, the old boy had died. A rough-looking gang brought a truck, which they parked in Albert Street and stripped the shelves, while Piers looked on distraught.

As if that was not enough, Mother committed the ultimate betrayal and married a man from Church. Piers moved out and built himself a nest of self-pity in a bedsit.

Routine makes cowards of us all. Who has not felt the sense of oppression when our daily habits become entrenched in a clutter of repetition? The freest spirit can succumb to it and the most intrepid find, in later years, a sudden unwillingness even to leave the house. Piers Farnaby had never been free. The paths he made wound ever tighter in an enveloping noose. That was how he liked it. He knew the circle of his thoughts. Felt comfortable with his woes. As a victim of his own contriving, he therefore found it difficult to adjust to the possibility of having a friend.

One day, as he was hurrying down Market Street, past the open-fronted fish stalls, - pink crabs crawling amidst the piles of winkles and prawns - he was accosted by a strapping fellow with a mop of chestnut hair.

"Piers Farnaby!" exclaimed this giant, slapping him on the shoulder. "I'd know you anywhere. How are you, you sly old devil!"

Piers visibly cowered.

"Oh, come on. Don't tell me you've forgotten? Nigel. Nigel Henslow. We were in the same class at School."

Of course Piers remembered. This ruffian led the gang of tormentors who had pulled his hair and scribbled over his books when he was small.

"Those were the days, eh? What are you up to now? Come for a drink and tell me. We're two of a kind, we are. Home boys. Everyone else has gone away. We must stick together!"

Piers had no wish to stick to anyone but he found himself hustled into The Golden Fleece and deposited on a stool by the bar.

"*Don't drink?*" spluttered his new companion. "My God! You really haven't changed. Two lagers, my darling," he said to the barmaid, "and something for yourself." And he pulled out of his pocket a roll of five pound notes, fat as his fist.

"I'm in antiques!" he announced, broadcasting the confidence to the world. "What about you? *Clerical assistant?*" There was no mistaking his tone of mockery. "Good for you! It's a funny thing about antiques - we're a close family - at least - those of us who trade on the 'invisible' side. My firm now, we're ordinary 'knockers' by day. But we've got relatives everywhere. Some of the most respected establishments are cousins of ours. We have a nice warehouse just below the station and a place in London too."

Piers had slunk past this warehouse on occasional trips out of town. There would be vans parked at the gate with open doors and enormous Chinese vases and strongmen and Alsatian dogs in possession of the pavement. Nigel, in his leather jacket, looked the part.

"Those relatives of mine cleared a shop for a friend of yours not long ago. Old Dawkins? The chess man in The Lanes? We've got some of his stock. I thought I must come and tell you, right away."

So this was no chance encounter. It was another ambush. Piers, gripped his glass and looked around for the door.

"It's all right, Mummyboy." Nigel used that hateful playground tag with glee. "We can be true friends now. I've got news that is going to change your life."

Someone had been talking behind his back. Someone who knew him must have shopped him. Set him up. Brandrith! Piers backed away, his chin trembling with anger and shame.

But Henslow had now dropped his voice and began musing almost to himself: "Dawkins. Now *there* was a funny chap. He used to buy stuff from us, you know. Oh yes. We supplied him with some of his best sets. He never asked where they came from and he always paid on the nail. That was, until he got involved with the piece from Samarkand. That one purchase changed everything for him. He became a recluse and virtually shut up shop."

"What do you mean?" said Piers, unable to hold back.

Nigel didn't hear or ignored him all the same. "We didn't understand it at the time. We went on supplying him, thinking he'd get himself straight again, but the man was so possessed with that thing he got into hopeless debt. He went on buying, but what was he doing with the stuff? Just hoarding it? Or cheating us and selling it on? Rumours about his oddness began to fly."

"Everybody was curious," said Piers. "And nobody knew what finally became of him. They said that he had died but there was no official notice - no funeral, and the shop is *still* there, with the original sign and the metal grill at the window. It used to be one of the smartest shops in The Lanes. Now it is empty, almost derelict. I saw it myself the day after he died. They raided his shop in broad daylight."

Nigel regretfully shook his head and sighed. "Necessary measures I'm afraid. The executors would never have handed our merchandise back. There were other creditors you see and some of that stuff had... special pedigree."

"You stole it?"

"*Saved* it. But the good news is that it is now on the market again. Are you interested? Drink your drink first and think about it. I'm not talking about the chess sets only, lovely as they are. There are other things. Papers. Letters. Even a diary of sorts. His research went pretty deep. He was prepared to take quite extraordinary risks."

"Was he *murdered*?" said Piers, aghast.

"You'd have to judge for yourself." Henslow knocked back the last of his beer and, knowing he had said enough, rose as if to go.

The bait was working already. And Piers, though every shred of reason warned against it, found himself unable to resist. Collector's craving is as potent as any drug. The chance of acquiring something new intoxicates the brain and triggers a chain of reactions, addictive in themselves. True collectors, like gamblers, know the mental agitation, the physical constriction of the heart, the irritability, the illogical justifications which accompany every pursuit. Collectors experience all the thrills of a love affair: desire, despair, the thrill of acquisition. and then the momentary satisfaction, the complacency and sometimes the disgust which will bring the thing full circle. Each love is the true one, as necessary to existence as food or air. Each love is worth the ultimate sacrifice and any attempt at rational restraint is destined to be swiftly overthrown. Piers knew that Henslow meant disaster. He knew that only a fool would put any trust in him. He was not such a fool. He would not get involved in dubious business.

That morning he had been content with life. What old Dawkins knew had been no concern of his. He had all but forgotten the man. But now a narcotic curiosity was itching away in his blood. What would he miss if he really turned away? Fate had offered him this opportunity. It might be cowardly, not to say ungrateful, to refuse. After all, he believed it was his special destiny to gather up and care for beautiful things. And had he not always hankered after the very items which were now flaunted as 'available'. What would become of them, if he did not rescue them? He could picture

51

Dawkins' sets quite clearly in his mind: the ivory and the jade; the wooden men, spelter men, soapstone and clay. He wanted possession of them *all*, not to mention this new and mysterious piece Nigel mentioned, the one too private and precious to display. Would they vanish forever in the criminal underworld? Or be broken up as trash? And what would become of the secrets they carried with them? Maybe he could not unlock those secrets yet. But he did not doubt they would reveal themselves to one who showed the necessary skill and patience. They had survived whole dynasties, empires - seen civilizations come and go. They had been traded and gossiped-over across the world. And who better to guard them now than a man who, from earliest youth, had conversed with kings? Dawkins must have failed, not being up to the task, but Piers was different. Piers was special. His mother had said so and Mother knew. And this wisdom would confer just the advantage he needed to triumph over scum like Nigel Henslow. He began to hunger for such deep and dangerous things. And the fear of letting them slip beyond reach brought on a slavish capitulation.

"I couldn't pay!" he gasped, catching at Henslow's sleeve. "Not all at once, I couldn't."

Henslow smiled. "No worries. Didn't I say you were my friend? You can do it on the never-never. Just like Dawkins. But you'll want to see the stuff before you decide."

"No I'll have it! I know I want it. I'll give you a deposit now if you like. I get my wages on Friday."

Nigel smiled with his teeth. "Where can I find you, Farnaby? Where do you live? I'll bring you an inventory and see how we go from there."

Piers lived at the top of a terraced house, set back from the Lewes Road. Down below, the buses plied back and forth, ferrying people in and out of the suburbs. It was a dirty, dingy road - a November afternoon of a road - full of tired women with shopping bags and hearses and loafers from bookie shops. Nearby, were the hidden crescents of finer and older houses and the elm trees of The Level, so splendid before the Dutch disease laid seige. There was Barry's church. And row upon row of slate roofs, which armoured the hillside, all the way from the old workhouse hospital to the

Victorian viaduct. The flat, with its attic windows, gave onto a back-door platform, from which a cast iron fire-escape dog-legged down till it finally reached the ground. Here Piers had always felt secure and free. He gave out his address with a sinking heart. But the current of destiny was gathering pace. He could feel it lift and sweep him along. Resistance was out of the question.

"Top floor. Number Two," he said. "You'll come, you promise?"

"Of course I'll come. I shall need to in any event." Henslow winked and threw out as if it were an aside: "After all, I am your landlord."

When Piers looked back upon this scene, he saw his whole life as a game of chess. Every move he made seemed to have been anticipated by an invisible adversary. Every blow for independence bound him more tightly to an inevitable end.

He became a thrall to the devious Henslow, who showered favours on him as he picked him clean.

The affable villain would arrive at the end of the day, with a bottle of something tucked beneath his arm. Under pretext of planning improvements he made regular inspections of the flat. He wished to know the lay-out of each room and how they tallied with the rooms below. Who cleaned the stairs? Who tended the shrubs in the yard? He expressed concern about the fire-escape and fitted new smoke alarms. And with a teasing relish, as though feeding treats to a dog, he brought out, pawn by pawn, the treasures of Dawkins' collection. When he had gone, Piers laid out his acquisitions, dusted them, wrapped them in silk, devised ever more elaborate boxes to store them in, and wrote out index cards in coloured pen: red for Asia, green for Europe, yellow for the Far East, for these were the joys of the true collector. That the pieces were 'hot' somehow added to their fascination. They were bound uniquely to the purchaser.

The papers - Dawkins' private scribbling - were thrown in virtually gratis. Here were notes upon everything, from opening gambits to endgames, from variants to innovations and copious pages devoted to something called 'Shahmats', a peculiar form of the game for a solo player.

Computer chess has made the concept of solo contests commonplace. But 'Shahmats', a corruption of the Persian for 'checkmate', with its original meaning *'the King is dead'*, was a mystic, psychological version, according to Dawkins, a heresy which was promptly banned by all later adherents of logic and deduction. 'Shahmats', in effect, could not have been played by a computer. It did not involve a selection of options - this path or that? - but rather, an open invitation to the unknowable. In 'Shahmats' the solo player selected spirits to challenge one another. A special mental detachment was required to prepare a void into which their vital energies could be drawn. Those same energies directed the field. In a development of his own devising, Dawkins proposed to pitch himself against a spirit antagonist. He would set out his pieces, play his move and retire to bed. By morning, his opponent would have responded. This psychic chess was to be played at propitious times of the solar calendar, but contacting the departed proved more difficult than he at first supposed. Some pieces turned out to be more receptive than others to psychic influence and he was unable to identify with any precision what that 'influence' was. The dangers of engaging in such activity should have been self-evident. Why else was the game originally suppressed? No reputable chess-master had even heard of it. Yet Dawkins rejected conventional chess as a degenerate form, insisting that 'Shahmats', the 'great game', as he called it, was the true one and that its aim was nothing less than the acquisition and exercise of spiritual power.

He recorded his games, move by move, in his diary and this document became a kind of Holy Scripture for his young disciple. Piers read it through obsessively, replaying each manoeuvre, seeking new clues. There had been games between Indian princes, games between Arab and Turk, Moor against Spaniard, and all along the Silk Road into China, armies battling for victory. The prize? Nothing less than access to cosmic 'mysteries'. The Persians, so he read, had mastered these mysteries in the eleventh century and a secret order of initiates passed the knowledge down, with directions, encrypting everything from statecraft to the motions of the stars.

That Dawkins himself came close to unlocking the very same truths Piers did not for one moment doubt, for his disappearance took place during a most significant game.

Let me explain. The prize of Dawkins' collection was a solitary piece of exceptional antiquity. This piece was made of ivory and, so Henslow assured him, had an impeccable provenance. Unquestionably, it had seen better days. Some details were broken but enough survived to identify it as an Indian-style charioteer. In the Indian precursor to chess, many pieces took elaborate forms with characters on elephant- and camel-back. The elephant underwent a drastic change when Islam imposed its ban on images. In the severely abstract sets of the Muslim world, a pair of tiny tusks was all that remained of its once-majestic form. And these tusks, resembling the tips of a bishop's mitre, gave Western chess its Bishop. Such transformations were commonplace. The fastest piece on the 'Chatranj' board was the charioteer, which speakers of Farsi knew as Rokh. So, Rokh became Rook and Rook became Castle in the modern game.

This particular Rook turned up in Holland Park in the house of a Turkish Jew, being one of the treasures his family kept when they left Medieval Spain. Mordecai Marks, the last of the line, died without heir and many of his possessions, the ivory rook among them, made the dubious journey to a storehouse in Islington, which is where Nigel Henslow spotted it. He brought it down to Brighton.

Dawkins saw at once that this was something special - one of the earliest chessmen, perhaps, in the world. It bore, so he said in his excitement, the hallmark of Sogdian design, which meant that it had come from Samarkand.

Samarkand! The very name breathed excitement. Samarkand meant poetry and the spice of adventure - a metaphor for greatness - for it was once quite reasonably believed that whoever ruled Samarkand, would have mastery of the world. Few could have doubted it, and the murals of the ancient King's palace clearly showed it, with merchants bringing tribute from every corner of the earth. Even Farnaby knew that.

Those murals, had been dug out of desert dust barely ten years before Dawkins met his end. He must have known it too, (why else should he have chosen Afrasiab to be his final adversary?) for it was this Turanian king, Persia's great enemy, who gave his name to the hill where the palace stood.

Scholars, delving into the name Afrasiab - a compound of Old Persian and Tajik words - translate it as: '*beyond the black river*'. And yes, to be sure, there *was* a river there, innocently curving to the north. But when it came to Afrasiab the man, a warrior who famously aligned himself with the powers of darkness, then the name suggested something more sinister. For Afrasiab had set his heart on nothing less than destruction through sorcery. A fight with that regicide would be a fight to the death. Or perhaps a fight with death itself? What *was* the black river and what truly lay beyond? Did anyone ever learn and live to tell? Did Dawkins do it? Suppose such a thing *could* be done? The prize might be immortality. If Piers could only find out for himself what happened in that final, fatal game, he would make his mark in the annals of chess forever. He would enter the realms of legend - rout the common rabble he so despised and take his place with the likes of Babur and Tamburlane. *Then* Mother would see...

He pored over his books into the early hours. He read Persia's ancient poets and gradually came to suspect that the ultimate game of 'Shahmats' might be a game with Dawkins himself. But first dispatch the Turanian...

Throughout all this, he maintained an air of utmost secrecy. He worked on quietly at the bank, earned his promotion, learned to use computers and handed over most of his pay each week to the predatory Henslow. It has to be said that Piers did not feel used. He felt, in a curious way that Henslow was serving him. The man could not have guessed the importance of what he was doing. Or could he?

He continued to buy his victim drinks, introduced him to his sister, who lived nearby, and steadily fuelled his insatiable addiction. Alison Henslow soon wormed her way into Farnaby's confidence with a blend of interest and sympathy. On dreary afternoons they would meet in the transport cafe just along from The Working Mens' Club and Piers discovered a poignant source of pleasure in unburdening his afflicted soul to her. Soon he had told her all about his past, his mother's betrayal and how the girls at work laughed behind his back. Alison cooed and tutted and smoothed his ruffled feathers. When he went down with the 'flu she made him soup. And once inside his flat, she began to clean and tidy for him, just as Mother used to do. Of course he was discreet at first. He locked the door of the 'chess' room and hid his books. Alison was often unhappy, too. Her husband had run off. Her life had been fraught by misadventure. She had no friends and she was half afraid of her brother. She was as dull and homely as Nigel was debonair.

One evening in November, Piers made the fatal mistake of talking about 'Shahmats'. Alison instantly begged to see his collection. She asked an endless stream of questions and flattered Piers by suggesting he was 'chosen'. Now was the time, she urged, to put 'Shahmats' to the test. A game begun before Christmas might prove things one way or the other. She would help him, she promised. Two heads were better than one. She would bring him supper and together they would issue a challenge which the spirit of Afrasiab could not refuse.

Night after night, as the Christmas lights rolled out across the town, they sat up late with a bottle of wine between them. Should they be black or white? Which set to use? Which version of the game? The piece from Samarkand decided for them. Since he was white they chose to play with him and since Tamerlane Chess originated from Turania, they made up the ranks with hybrid 'fairy' pieces: leaping giraffes and oxen and archers on horseback. If they were to play this game of 'perfect chess', they would have the finest troops to fight it out. With a breathless sense of daring they arranged the board, decided on an opening move, retired and locked the door. Alison returned to her flat and Piers sank into a sleep like the sleep of the dead.

The following morning they were electrified to find that one black pawn had moved. Neither could wait for dusk to play again and make a bid for the centre of the board. There followed another night of deep oblivion and daylight revealed a black knight on the move. All day, Piers tried to read the enemy mind. Should he make an open attack, or play for subtlety, lure his opponent on, bide time

57

and lie in wait? Those years of suffering surprise attacks had surely taught him something... So the game progressed. But no matter what he did, the spirit across the water seemed to know. Piece by piece, as Christmas time drew near, his forces dwindled round his precious king. He lost the will to eat. He skimped his work. He all but barred his door to the anxious Alison. He kept his curtains drawn, barricaded the French windows. Locked in deadly choreography, the rival's forces countered each attack but even when he vowed to watch and wait, Piers never managed to see how it was done. Each night he fell into oblivion and did not wake until the following day.

Christmas passed and Piers now took on the look of a man condemned. Trapped by his own neurosis, he had the appalling sense that everything he thought was known already. The eyes of the other side, it seemed, saw all. Fear took possession of his soul. Each new day brought a sickening dread, which Alison's sympathy only intensified. If he was to lose, and meet whatever fate was due, then he must do that hateful thing alone. At last he refused to open his door at all. Three days before Christmas, notice came that the vintage fire-escape was to be removed. New smoke alarms had rendered it redundant and the rusting structure posed a security risk. The noise of metal-grinding was more than flesh could bear and Piers, who had skipped going in to work for a week, roamed about the streets till the job was done. When he came back, he found his door ajar. Alison, her white face streaked with tears, told him a gang had been. Raided the flat and looted his collection. Someone had tipped them off.

But the game? The game was up. Elephants, grand viziers, the whole lot had been taken.

Piers stood stunned. Should he go to the Police? What could he say to the Police? All his life's earnings, his hopes, his plans, his trust, had been obliterated at a blow. Nothing remained but the Turanian Rook which he had always kept in his pocket and which, with its queer, lopsided smile now seemed to mock at him. He had been a fool - allowed himself to be abused again. He did not doubt that Nigel Henslow had once more been his undoing. Alison put her hands upon his shoulders.

"Not Nigel," she sobbed. "He's not to blame. It was me!"

"You?"

"Yes, I was a plant. Don't look at me like that. I know it was wrong. It was my job to encourage you and help you play the game. It was my job to copy your keys and drug your wine so that Nigel could come up to make his move as soon as you were asleep. I reported our manoeuvres - noted them down and he worked out the response. It was all a game to him. It tickled his depraved idea of fun. He always had been horribly jealous of you. Lord alone knows why - you are such a funny thing. But Nigel's cruelty has a criminal edge. He had done this all before with the old boy in The Lanes. He let him gamble all his stock on this one crazy game and when it came to checkmate the shock of it - the realisation of all he had lost brought on a heart attack. You were different. It's harder to scare a younger man to death and then, suppose you won? You *are* a formidable player, you know. No, if he was going to recover his stock and work the scam again, he'd have to make sure of you before the end. It was *my* idea to remove the fire-escape and steal the collection once you were out of the house. It was my key which let his henchmen in. I'd like to say I'm sorry, but I'm not. I'd rather you lost the lot than died for it."

She dropped her hands and shrank against the wall. "It's crazy I know, but I've become really fond of you. I'd like to think one day you could be happy. This chess - this 'Shahmats' rubbish - don't you see, it's been destroying you?"

Piers blinked as the meaning of her words sank in.

"It was killing you!" she groaned. "And it was all nonsense, cooked up, like a wicked schoolboy prank. It has cost one man his life already. I couldn't bear to see that happen to you!"

"You mean there really was no 'Shahmats'...?"

"Nigel made it up. He wrote the diary - he's good at that kind of thing. He could have gone somewhere, made something of his life if he hadn't been such a beast."

"And you..."

"I told you I was scared of him. I shan't go into it but you have to believe I'm not the same as him. As soon as I realised you really needed me, I wanted to set you free."

59

"And why shouldn't I turn you in and make you pay? There are laws you know..."

"No reason," she replied. "Except you could find yourself better things to do. Even if you had survived the 'Shahmats' game, what would you have become without my help? A solitary, sad, embittered loser. No friends. No family. Just sores and old, unsettled scores."

"And what shall I be now that you have *liberated* me?" He pushed her away and found he rather enjoyed it.

"Forget it." She held out her hands again. "Forget about being special. Just be human. It's not too bad. You could get to like it." But he was no longer listening. Some new idea had sowed itself in the furrow of his mind. Some new possibility...

"What shall we do, then?"

"Start again..." she said, her eyes suddenly shining.

"You know he will be back?"

"Yes, yes I know. He's got the key. He'll want the final piece."

"We'll leave it for him where he cannot miss it. And we'll hide in here and see just what he does."

"Let him have it. It's no use to us."

"Oh yes," said Piers with a quiet determination. "I shall let him have it!"

And they set the ivory charioteer on a damaged board which Nigel had left behind, turned off the lights and concealed themselves in the adjacent room. And whether Piers at last succumbed to the warmth of her caresses and whether he opened the little door of his heart may never now be known. At ten to twelve a key turned in the lock. A torch-beam flashed for a moment beneath the door. The intruder made for the living room and they heard a satisfied sigh as he spotted his prize. Piers stood transfixed, his eyes staring as though they could pierce the wall. They heard a movement and then a sound they could not place at first, which seemed to come from a great way off. And perhaps it was not a sound so much as a vibration, felt through every fibre, as insistent and inexorable as the march of a distant army. Yes, the sound of something approaching, with an inexorable purpose. The sound of someone climbing the fire-escape - the fire escape *which was no longer there...* Nigel must have heard it too for he had stopped dead in his tracks. Piers could feel it with an exultant joy. 'Shahmats' was not a sham. Something steadfast and appalling was approaching across the river of darkness in which they all lay enisled... Coming to claim its prize...

In his mind's eye he could already see a hand on the balcony door. And at that very moment a ghastly cry, an unearthly howl of naked horror rent the air. Alison later made a stammering attempt to describe the sound, but found that she could not. Nor could she describe the whimpering which followed. She had frozen with fear, but Piers, Piers had somehow grown in stature and towered above her in a dreadful way. He it was who seized her hand and marched her into the room where a blaze of light revealed the scene of a struggle. The chessman was gone. The balcony door gaped wide. One of Nigel's shoes lay shredded on the carpet.

How to explain such things to the authorities, or to the men who later took charge of Piers was beyond a simple girl like Alison. It seemed this game had finally played itself out and all she could say was: "They were so like each other. So hell-bent on what they wanted. Why couldn't they just be nice to one another?"

The detective sergeant got her a cup of tea. When it was all over, he thought, he might ask her out for dinner.

The significance of the case was equally lost on the team at the mental asylum.

"He is quite convinced he has summoned up a king from Samarkand. Most interesting delusions..."

But the truth? The truth was maybe something more bizarre...

*Oh mighty Afrasiab, tell me, was it **you**, playing destiny with human pawns? Was it you, wasting life upon the sand? And who is now at the whim of your next move? We are shadows merely, indulging in shadow-play. And who decides whether we win or lose?*

"...for like the lightning to this field
I came, and like the wind I go away..."

61

The Other

The Other

At Mr. Wyndham's' dinner party?

I am astonished, my friend, that you have heard of it. True, there were celebrated figures there, not least Mr. Wyndham himself, who may be described as one of the last patrons of the Arts in the grand old manner. His house is always open, though hacks and fakes avoid it, fearing exposure amongst its regular visitors. I had never belonged to that circle - you see how even to speak of them inflates my language by association. I was ever one to mistrust high-flown words, my view being that bluster is nothing but a modesty towel to cover nakedness. As all who know me will affirm, I have a talent for spotting bunk. I can see through walls, which is to say, I can see what is generally hidden from view. So when I hear myself speak this way, I know how you will judge me. However that may be, I repeat, I was not one of *them*, and though Feakins, my old college friend, had been a regular visitor since his London exhibition brought him fame, it was only through him that I came to hear of Mr. Wyndham and of those intellectuals who surrounded him.

Men such as myself - the quieter sort of dreamers - belong in life's ante-rooms. We are not fit for banquets. We have small stomachs and the very thought of food is enough to fill us up. I should have stood forever outside, content to wait and spend my days in gentle pining after the indigestible, and so I *would* have done, to my own pleasing mortification, had it not been for this dinner party.

You must understand that my whole life has been an exercise in procrastination. Insignificant I may be, but I have never lost sight of the hope that one day my true worth would come to light. Once I had visionary moments, as all children do: autumnal spider webs and summer leaf-patterns exercised over me their usual enchantments. But it has been my secret comfort to watch the waning of such experience in others who clutter their lives up with material rubbish, while feeding within myself the latent spark of that by which the world might be transformed.

Spiritual power! I see you look at me askance, but I have nurtured this thought through all my adult years. I have, yes, cultural ambitions, frustrated though they are by a lack of confidence. I can write, less pompously than this, when I choose. I can draw with some ability. I am well-read in several languages. I have had a gentleman's education and though I cannot catch a ball, I can play the clarinet rather better than most. Yet I excel at nothing. I make no money. Achieve no recognition.

"If only Christian here would put his mind to it..." I feel Feakins clap me on the back, "he could do almost anything."

Could... could... *would*. Ah, the blessed conditional tense! Would I had stayed in it, there, and in the subjunctive, forever!

For their part, it seemed better that everyone should believe in my dormant abilities. For my own, I suppose I was afraid that such skills might fail me if actually put to the test, or worse, that their fulfilment might overpower the subtler gift I nursed at their expense - my private power of dreaming. You will laugh at the sacrifices I made. - the opportunities I let slide by, all with the silent promise upon my lip that one day I would bring power to play. A respectable career, marriage with - words, slow your pace - a girl who was altogether my match and other things here and there - openings, journeys, adventures, children... I watched *others* enjoy them and relished the pangs of envy until the very possibility of having them slipped out of sight.

"You throw yourself away!" says Feakins, pouring coffee from the percolator. "Come and make something of your life."

As I turn homewards in the dusk, a glimmer of light from my window warms my heart and I think of myself, alone, outside and free and able to defer commitment indefinitely. Such have I been, a devotee of art and books with a passion for porcelain; a passive friend; an unassuming cat's paw, jealously concealing all trace of the spiritual impatience and arrogance that smoulders within. So would I have been until my cousin, or my few acquaintances buried me with a dutiful oration.

But you are asking of Mr. Wyndham's party...

It was an evening in September, the sky clear, the sunlit air heavy with golden dust. Shadows were long. I had been walking along the river and was returning home in solitary contemplation, when I heard hurried footsteps at my back and turning, beheld old Feakins, dressed in style.

"Wherever are you going?"

"Where, but to Mr. Wyndham's," he replied, slotting his hands into his linen pockets.

I must have snorted in an offhand manner, to which he, unfortunately took offence, and striking an attitude there in the street, accused me of inverted snobbery. I hotly defended myself, though I admit my defence was weak, and the upshot was that he challenged me either to go along with him and prove an open mind, or go to the Devil and forget we had ever been friends. He was naturally volatile and on this night particularly so on account of a row with his wife. To humour him, I abandoned my own plans and allowed myself to be led, my mind blank at the thought of what lay ahead.

Let me explain. I have never been smart, or in any way distinguished in my attire, preferring, save for a brief fling with a Homburg, to cultivate an anonymous appearance. Now, dressed as I was for a stroll, I cut a poor figure beside my friend in his fancy leather brogues. Given one moment to reflect, I might have guessed I would look wildly out of place, yet Feakins, in the heat of his irritation, marched me up the steps and pushed me into the house with so much force, I was unable to remonstrate until I was in the room and facing the company.

A stooped, emaciated, elderly man with a whitening beard came towards us and said in a musical voice:

"Mr. Bernadetti, *what* a pleasure. What a pleasure! We have asked Edward so often to bring you, hearing of your many accomplishments. We have started to eat, so I will dispense with introductions which are always so tedious. Your name is familiar to us in any case."

He pressed my hand with a limp, dry hand of his own, singularly unpleasing in its grasp, and nodding to Feakins with a smile, led me towards a table laden with food.

What struck me immediately was that the guests, already seated, behaved as though they were at some Florentine court or French salon, rather than at an ordinary party. Conversation was conducted by strict rules: one person only to speak at a time and to address the whole gathering. No private tittle-tattle. And no flippancy either. Thoughtfulness was all. Quite contrary to my expectations, it was skill in this matter which took pride of place. And so dazzled was I by the effect, it took me some time to appreciate the room itself and the crowd of people in it. Men and women, dressed with casual elegance, mixed easily together, while waiters discreetly filled their plates and encouraged them to eat, drink and be merry.

Nobody noticed me and I soon felt strangely at ease. I recognized some famous men of letters, a pianist, an explorer, whose name escaped me. And all the time I had the novel sensation of inhabiting the present and *enjoying* it. *Tomorrow*, I promised myself, *tomorrow I will be quiet and return to my solitary ways*.

The meal once cleared away, the port arrived and coffee and chocolate-coated wafers on silver trays. Here and there - remember that we are all ghosts now and this all happened in a different age - arabesques of smoke curled up from smiling lips. Somebody opened the spinet and began to play.

Mr. Wyndham let his intelligent gaze pass over his guests and by this token alone showed his delight.

"What shall it be - an evening of pure pleasure, or of debate?"

'Pure pleasure' sounded an unnerving prospect, but I was spared any further alarm on that account for the company wished to talk, and to my relief, decided to talk about dreams - a subject with which I was familiar. It was agreed that each guest in turn should speak before the floor was opened to all. I have never been any use at this kind of thing. The very notion of public speaking fills me with dread. Prayer meetings, party games - it is all the same. I loathe them. I contrive to be last, vainly hoping that Fate will step in and spare me. But cowardice never pays. My turn will come and by the time it does, there will be nothing left to say. However, this evening things were different. I listened with enjoyment to my fellow guests. And much to my own surprise, I found myself smiling as Feakins ended his speech and the faces of the assembly turned towards me.

"It is affirmed by de Quincey," I began, pitching in rather fast and unnaturally high, "that the skill of magnificent dreaming was in decline even before the Victorian Age. His own addiction to opium he defended sometimes in these terms, that while allaying physical pain, it also satisfied that need for potent dreams, which distinguishes us from the lower animals. The days of the 'opium eater' are over. Today our dreams have been kidnapped by commercial enterprise. They are pressed into service for mere advertisements, while the world forgets their true and sacred function."

My voice carried over the heads of the crowd and seemed a comforting thing, for it had fallen in pitch and now flowed in a measured pace. From de Quincey I ranged to the Aborigines, who believed that the Earth was dreamt into existence; from them to Yeats who held that the imagination could figure forth symbols with material power...

At length, the voice I had been listening to ceased to speak and there followed a longish, gratifying silence. Then someone, unexpectedly, raised an objection. There were points to clarify... Could it be that all I had stated with such confidence would now be pulled apart?

"They are not conjectural theories," I replied, "but Truth. For every life there is also a dream life which is a spectral shadow of what might be. Every one of us has known visionary moments, when both lives overlap. I am not speaking of wishing or day-dreaming, but of an antithetical duality - much like the dream table Plato envisaged as a spiritual counterweight to the table a common carpenter makes of wood."

"But are you suggesting that there can be some positive, not merely perceptual link between the two?" asked a young woman, whose hair was shorn at the back.

I faltered, and for a moment feared that I was lost, but Feakins unexpectedly came to my rescue.

"Inasmuch as the dream of a perfect table influences a carpenter, surely the glimpse of a fully realised life has a positive influence upon us when we dream."

"I don't mean that at all," said I, picking up my thread with renewed conviction. "I do not speak of a pattern or code - some celestial copy-book. I mean a parallel reality which simply *exists*. And where things enjoy a parallel existence, they may, may they not confront one another?"

"Is it of dreams we are speaking, or of ghosts?" asked the pianist.

"Perhaps that is a matter of words only," said Mr. Wyndham, his eyes excitedly shining. "And words, as every Humpty Dumpty knows, are neither here nor there. They mean whatever we choose."

Once more I felt they had taken things out of my hands. How dare they twist my words so lightly this way and that? Accustomed to my own slow measure of thought, I was unable to hold my own. I made a lame reply and somebody who laughed was taken to task, for in that world the rules of etiquette were clear. Derision, when it came, and come it *would*, was something to be saved and savoured in privacy.

"Let us make a scientific experiment," said the pianist, while I sulked in silence. "Let us try what Mr. Yeats prescribed, or what de Quincey failed to do without his drugs - our own measure of magnificent dreaming. Let each of us, when we leave tonight, imagine some symbol, or figure, or action with our whole power of concentration and observe whether anything comes of it."

There was an appreciative spate of laughter. Despite my dull-wittedness, it seemed, I had become the darling of the evening. But I did not forget those moments of defeat and a seed of resentment sprouted in my soul.

Feakins left in high spirits, having forgotten the affair with his wife.

"You were *very* funny, old man. You were a great success! Promise you'll come to the next."

We had reached the corner of the Quadrant, the boundary of my narrow neighbourhood. Beyond lay the streets where I spent my bachelor days - a shop-browsing life of teacups and window-boxes and hours in which the declining sun drew horological shadows round the chimney pots.

Eager to escape, I shook my head and glanced at him with a refusal on my lips and then, at the sight of his corduroys and jocund face, I experienced an unexpected change of heart. The voice which had spoken with confidence hours before assented on my behalf from *choice*, not as I might have done, from laziness.

Now I forget how we parted, remembering only the daze in which I completed my journey home. Passing the lighted shops, I forgot to count my customary landmarks - tree, lamp, pillar-box - all to be noted, each in its place. The street itself dissolved in a blur of emotion which I can only equate with my brief taste of love.

Yet love this most certainly was *not*. When I looked back upon the evening as a whole, my overall sensation was one of controlled disgust. It was the very feeling I had felt on taking Mr. Wyndham's hand. There had been something tastelessly artificial about it all. A lethal insincerity...

I need not go, I murmured as I let myself into the hall - and again - climbing the stairs: *What foolish nonsense. Let me forget it all. In the morning it will seem, as it was, unreal.*

My room overlooks a street lined with lofty plane trees which branch to the sky and obscure large sections of the houses opposite. On summer evenings the sun lingers late amongst the leaves while the street below is cold. On winter nights, the lamp-light gleams through a halo of rain-wet branches. Here I sit in the high window with nothing for company but a terra cotta griffin which grins from a neighbouring rooftop. I had made a companion of the thing for years. It sat, in snow, in sun, unseen by passers-by, a creature like myself, wrapped in its secret life - my metaphor. I looked on it as a soul-mate, which perhaps explains why I dreamt of it that night.

Some creature - I know not what - was hunting in the foliage of the plane tree. I could hear the rustle of its wings and the soft, moaning cry as it hovered close. And seized with a horrible, choking fear, I groped for my shoe and hurled it from the window.

I could not see what happened in the dark. I heard something - a crash below - and threw myself under the blankets.

Next morning I was surprised to find my window open. Rain had blown in and soaked the rug. My griffin was gone from its perch.

Frequently, during the day, I felt the wish to be revenged upon Mr. Wyndham and his fawning coterie. Raise a ghost after all? As I had shown last night, I had read about it all. Conjuration! What else is poetry but the action of the mind, summoning forms out of nothing? Surely it would be a simple step to add corporeal substance... I did not doubt my ability to do it. And such a stunt would certainly prove my worth to the Wyndham crowd. Yet with each temptation I became the more convinced there was something sinister in it, something verging on the criminal, which would harm my soul. Time and again I put temptation aside and returned to my affairs with a sense of relief. My anger waned. I busied myself all day, arranging my collection of Meissen ware. A letter from my landlord renewed my lease and I retired early to bed and slept the sleep of the just.

This pattern of life continued for several days. Applying myself to humble tasks, I felt a sense of well-being such as I had not known, for years. I wrote to Feakins excusing myself from any further parties.

Then, late one night, I was roused from sleep by someone at the door. The ringing was violent and persistent, and though I got up, I did not dare to answer. The night was rough and I feared there might be drunks abroad.

The visitor at length gave up and I returned to bed.

In blustered Feakins the following day. He had received my letter and was full of reproach.

"*And* you ignored me last night," he added, maintaining an injured tone. "I know you were up because I saw you at the window. I call that unfriendly, Christian."

Unable to make any sense of his words, I merely stammered that it was late and that I did not answer the door after nine o'clock.

Feakins pursed his lips. "And what were you doing anyway?" He rested the rim of his coffee cup on his lower lip. "Most unlike you to be up at all."

"I was writing an article," I lied, feeling it might be better to humour him than risk having another disagreement. "And you? What did you want, in any case?"

"I was checking up on you, old man," said he. "Somebody, and I forget now who it was, told me you had refused my invitation to accept another from Mireille."

"Mireille!" I cried in astonishment, upsetting my drink. "Whatever put that idea into your head?"

Feakins looked greatly embarrassed and said that he must have had misheard and realised it when he saw my lamp. No hard feelings?

None. Only I did beseech him not to discuss me with his friends. The image of Mireille and her dark-haired daughter rose up to reproach me. Visit her? I? There could be no chance of seeing her ever again.

"It was she who put in the window boxes, you know," I said, letting my thoughts run on. "She insisted that one must never mix pink and orange flowers as careless gardeners do. I still cling to her advice."

"Mmm?" He too was thinking. "I'm sorry. It was a tactless thing to say. It's just that I never could understand your letting her go."

"Peace and quiet. I needed peace and quiet."

"For what?"

"Well, for... for all sorts of things. It wouldn't have worked. She knew she could never change me. She did much better with that Scottish engineer."

Feakins looked grave. "He beat her, you know. She had to get a divorce."

Though there was no way to explain it, I found that I already knew. I merely nodded back.

"Do you..." he let the question drop, but I finished it for him.

"Miss her? Not very much. I haven't the time."

73

"Christian, you are an idiot! You don't deserve to be happy. You should have stayed in academia and become a decayed professor."

"I know," I smiled. "No more tedious articles for 'China World'. But I haven't the patience to apply myself. Couldn't put my cards on the table. They did quite right to kick me out."

Feakins straightened the cushion in his chair, then rose, with a curious look I could not read, and abruptly left.

I could not help feeling glad, though I knew that some vital part of our friendship was leaving with him. He had, with his tiresome prodding stirred up a storm in the rock pool of my mind and it would take some time for the water to clear again.

I saw him off and it was not till my return that I noticed the thing which had so affected him. Protruding from the cushion in his chair was a brightly-coloured piece of cloth which I recognised. It was a scarf with peonies on it. I had no idea how it had come there but it belonged to *her*.

From that moment on, I felt I was slowly losing hold of the fabric of my life. Frosty shopkeepers began to hail me like a friend. The postman brought me goods I had not ordered. My telephone rang with calls from unknown callers, regarding things I knew I had not done. In an attempt to shake them off, I abjured all company and barred my door at seven.

I found my Homburg hat and took to wearing it, avoiding recognition in the street. My life, it seemed, detached from my consciousness, had assumed an enigmatic existence of its own.

One morning, I shuffled into the hall to find a pile of post: a letter from Feakins, thanking me for the loan of a book, a circular, offering me the instant chance to win a thousand pounds, and a formal note from University College, acknowledging my job application and inviting me to come for an interview.

"The book!" I cried. "My book!"

It was '*The Art of Memory*', a treasure I kept with other volumes of psychic interest. I *never* lend my books. It is a rule with me... I hurried to the shelves to find it gone. Inexplicably gone!

That day I began my packing, left the key with the agent, cancelled my lease, arranged for my belongings to go into store and decamped to the countryside.

Friend, I admit, in my college days, I have sat with others in the autumnal dusk, the wind whining and bothering outside, rose shoots tap-tapping at the window... There'd be a bottle of port, a book of some shocking phantasmagoria, passed from hand to hand and fear cosily seated in the cold core of the heart. I have frightened myself on winter nights and dismal afternoons in colleges, in castles, in churchyards, on moors and heaths, with all manner of ghouls and goblins. Such things are for the most part enjoyable.

But this unspecified threat of insanity on sunny mornings, in well-peopled streets, filled me with absolute terror.

At Ilfracombe, on the sands where I had once played as a child, I found respite. Stayed quietly at a guest house. Slept a lot. Gradually, I recovered and to my immediate relief, none of the symptoms of my Richmond nightmare followed. Indeed, I heard nothing at all. One day, as I walked by the sea, it occurred to me that I might as well be dead, for my present existence was one of numbing monotony. I walked, not for the love of walking, but to quiet my mind. I took sea air, oblivious to the motion of the waves or cries of seabirds overhead, simply to pass the time. I shed all interest, all attachment, all enquiry into the nature of things. I was at peace and perfectly moribund.

But the idea of death itself provoked a new line of thought, for death implies a previous life and my living thus, without question, in the present, must have been prefaced once by something else. Daily, I put anxiety aside - spent a little more of my capital. Daily, curiosity came back with a quiet insistence. How did they live without me? Did no one miss me at all? What was there now in the place of my griffin? Who looked out of the window and marked the shadows of the chimney pots?

This narrative had run from that fateful September evening until the beginning of March and I hardly knew myself.

Unable to still my nagging thoughts, I boarded the London train and made my way once more to Holbein Street. The house looked cheerful - spring bulbs at the windows - my own curtains neatly hanging at the windows. I thought how foolish I had been, running away at the first hint of trouble. This was my home and I felt happy here, just looking at the place and could not bring myself to leave again. Like a jail-bird at the prison gate, I hung about all day, haunting the streets and checking off the familiar landmarks as I went. Here was the pillar box where I posted my mail, here the gingko tree, here the Russian restaurant with its candelabra and little red horse in the window...

By dusk, I had returned to my original starting point. The house was dark and still I lingered on. It began to rain and a cavernous world opened up beneath the pavements. Lacquered reflections bobbed under the feet of passers-by. At length, feeling cold and tired, I pulled my collar up and turned my back to the wind. Here, came three jovial figures arm-in-arm, carelessly bumping into me. Two men and a woman. She even cast a look over her shoulder.

Without so much as an apology, they bundled in at my gate, opened the door and disappeared inside. Moments later, an upstairs light appeared, striking a pattern on the trunk of my tree. Then somebody crossed the room, peered into the street, and, brusquely drawing the curtains, blotted me out. How well I knew this scene from the other side! I knew the feel of the curtains. I knew every corner of the room, furnished still with its books and pictures as it had been when I lived there.

In the past it would have been *me* up there, - me imagining I saw some figure in the street below. In my strange, insulated world, this shadowy figure had been my constant companion. At night he liked to wait just where I now stood, a stranger beneath the lamp. He must have been my antithetical self. And it was comforting then to think he was watching me. Taking note of my furnishings and considering what impeccable taste I had... From the other side all was as it had always been - except that I was *here*. Outside. Unloved.

Glimpsing that figure at the window was like a physical blow. I had half-expected Feakins to be there, Mireille perhaps, but *you*!

I staggered back to the wall, with the hard, wet bricks behind me, then turned and hurried the length of Holbein Street. I would go back to Paddington, to the cliffs again, anywhere out of your sight!

You will tell me I was naïve to think I could exist without you. My mind is full of demons. They ransack my cupboards, pull out my few possessions, try on my clothes. As I speak, they are drinking my sherry. And reason? I have no use for reason now.

You ask, with casual interest, about Mr. Wyndham's party? That was your birthday and the day I began to lose my tangible existence. To whom, to what am I writing? Myself? My anti-self? My might-have-been? Laughing, with your arms around the woman who was mine? Living the life I was too craven to live? Who summoned you from exile? And what will happen to me now that you have usurped what once belonged to me? Shall I become a spectre in *your* mind's outlands - a revenant? *I shall not depart again*. How can you think I would?

I shall wait... feeling... searching for some way to get back in. However many times you shut me out, and pull the curtains tight, I shall still be there. I am the writing on the other side of the wall... What was, might be again...

Take care! A shift of tense, a chink is all I need... I am vigilant, vengeful... and I have all the time in the world!

The Language of Shadows

For K

The Language of Shadows

Yellow leaves. Russet leaves. The colours of an autumn kimono. That afternoon in late October, they met at the V & A and afterwards, arm-in-arm, trying to adjust to one another's pace, as novice lovers do, strolled beneath the trees in Kensington Gardens. And they had decided quite by chance to come to that particular museum, of all the museums in London, for their first rendez-vous. As unlikely a pair as you could wish to meet. Vincent Melchior had introduced them at his party and somehow, amidst the din of his designer set, they had discovered common ground: a taste for country walks and graveyards and the Hampstead sketches of John Constable, curries, Mahler, snow. They seemed to have inhabited the self-same worlds for half a life or more, leaving invisible footprints, side by side. And now, suddenly, there was this friendship, ready-formed - and more - a quickening of the pulse which youth and loneliness might precipitate into love.

Standing awkwardly, in front of the Japanese prints, they experienced a sudden sense of oneness - he, bespectacled, quiet, a dusty archivist, and she, flamboyant in her bright lipstick, a theatrical costume-maker - both were surprised, no overwhelmed by Hokusai's 'Great Wave', or rather by the force of colour in it. The prickling surge, with its layers of dazzling blue, towered, ready to seize, not only the struggling boats, which slid towards it, but the distant summit of Mount Fuji, too. It was as if the page itself discharged the needful catalyst to bring their souls together, raising a storm in the blood. Thus may a random conjunction of elements, a laboratory accident, change not only the experiment, but the world in which experiments are made. What more could an aspiring alchemist hope for?

The history of Prussian blue is a case in point. *If the pigment-maker Diesbach, back in 1705, had not been lazy and used a dirty glass, he would have produced the red that he intended. But one contaminating drop of Dippel's oil, a damned heretical oil – a reduction from the tomb - was enough to change that red to vibrant blue. Ecco! Hokusai had his wave.* Well, so it said in the curator's notes. And this same blue would in time infect the world with its extract of crumbled bone. Such chemistry could contaminate a well or inspire a masterpiece. And love - what was love, after all, but a transmutation of souls? A poison and an elixir, changing life, and death too, for all one knew, to the end of eternity.

Certainly, no one who saw the two of them, quietly scuffing leaves, would have guessed at the tumult of feeling beneath the skin - the nervous lightning, passing from hand to hand and electrifying the space between them. Young lovers are a common sight in London parks. What is so very special about it? Nothing. And when he looked back, Paul Manning could not even see the lovers. Instead he saw the colour of the day: yellow on flame; slate blue against rose pink. For from this day forward, that was how they would view the world.

In retrospect, he realised chance had nothing to do with it. What could have been more natural than that the miracle of Prussian blue should change their lives forever? He had come across Johann Dippel when researching notes for his *'History of Heresy'*. Born just too late for the Reformation, too soon for the Age of Reason, the man was a pietist turned necromancer. His life had been one long descent from grace. Obsessed with the dream of resurrecting life he had all but pawned his soul in the dissecting room. Imprisonment could not cure him. That his noxious oil, made from dead cats and heaven knew what besides, should be redeemed by an accident on an artist's mixing slab was a wonder all of its own. That Kate had her own connection to the tale, confirmed, a sense not merely of serendipity but of rightness - of everything coming together. Kate had, for weeks, been stitching robes for *'Lady Sarashina'*. The show was due to start in two weeks time and suddenly the production was in crisis. The director had had a change of heart. Wanting to add an apocalyptic note, he decided to set the action in the aftermath of Fuji's last eruption. He burnt the cherry trees - ripped up the costumes and stained them all with tea. The leading lady had refused to wear her wig, saying she was allergic to the smell, and there were complaints from health and safety about the ash. The cast were in an uproar and all Kate's work reduced to heaps of rags. But here, here on this wall, was a different Fujiyama, a series of snapshots that showed the mountain floating serenely capped with snow, wrapped in a lurid kimono of cloud as lightning danced below, dancing itself between the cherry leaves - Fuji drenched in a sea of colour as Sarashina might have seen it a thousand years before. And it was *colour* which formed the bridge on which one might dream life's sorrows away.

From that miraculous moment, the enraptured pair communicated in the language of colour. Days, moments, were turquoise and peach, red and aquamarine, according to their mood. And for Kate at least, love added a passion for everything Japanese. Their courtship was a strangely old-fashioned affair, spent mostly in galleries and suchlike public places. There was a flat at Kew however, and leisurely rambles round the Botanical Gardens which always ended with a trip to the Minka House, the traditional, Japanese farmhouse, grey amidst green bamboo.

Vincent Melchior's friends would have found the affair a hoot, and resented losing Kate to someone so prosaic. And Paul's fellow archivists would have frowned, thinking he was throwing his prospects away. Neither could talk to others about their love. Their secrecy defined them. Clandestine pleasures are the sweetest, so even after they were married, they kept their social and private lives apart, content to cultivate their difference. She loved nothing more than to explore the dusty corners of his mind. He gave her gravitas. His pragmatism provided a counterweight to her floating world. Sometimes he worried that they would share too much - arrive at a state of diffusive equilibrium. What would happen then? Would they grow bored with one another? With the very idea of love? Finally, he learned that it didn't matter. It was all one. And in any case there would be no time for getting bored.

Observing them on that first autumn day, could anyone have guessed how little time?

Japanese Art is the art of transience. Soon the autumn leaves are gone; the days grow short. Shadows lengthen. Here in the West we cling to permanence and stave off our winter dark with a barrage light. But memories fade faster than autumn leaves.

Now, when it mattered most, he could see the leaves, the lilac shadows of tree trunks on the grass, but her face eluded him. Of course there were photographs. Endless shots they had taken on their phones. That was not the same. He could not connect her eyes (were they grey or blue?) with her halo of hair or the little mole which floated above her temple. Her daylight self had gone. And instead he had to sit in the dark to picture her.

She would arrive exhausted from work with a box of sushi bought at a market stall. And often she had some present for him, some curio to make the room more like home. At first there were parasols and fans, a clutter of props, thrown out by the wardrobe department. All the rapture of discovery. As inexplicably, the clutter went out and instead she bought tatami mats and incense - a Japanese teapot. They tried a different tea each week - plum blossom - cherry - hibiscus. Whisked up thick, green, bitter-tasting matcha which they swallowed, laughing with a mutual shudder... They became connoisseurs, intoxicated by a kiss.

Then she had the news. An unassuming envelope. A casual appointment. A sentence delivered in a simple word.

The weariness which underlay her fragile joie de vivre was a lethal disorder of the blood. A letter summoned her to appointments and a gruelling course of treatment. White-walled rooms with the unremitting glare of fluorescent light. Waiting in corridors. Dizzying nausea. A total severance from the natural world.

When she came home, he filled the room with flowers and moved her chair to the window, trying to recreate the life they had shared before. But she had undergone a change. She did not want the brightly coloured shawls. She no longer craved a world of radiance. Instead she began to explore a new idea. She bought up lacquer-ware. Liquid black and red inscribed with gold designs. And when evening came the lovers lay, wrapped in the living dark and read together by the light of a paper lamp, while the flickering painted forms of carp and crane, pine-needles, crickets, moths, leapt from their lacquer grounds and filled in the air around them like burnished rhapsodies.

They breathed the scent of sandalwood from an incense-burner, fashioned like a miniature Minka House, the smoke rising in pale calligraphy from its chimney. The language of colour had gone and a new ideality appeared, a world of mouse grey tints - the language of shadows.

And he found it easier to reconstruct the curve of her cheek, the outline of brow or chin by the negative space which made flesh visible. Here was her smile, though you could not actually see it, held in place by the supportive void. He came to trust this void and then, without warning, she was gone.

Just as the doctors said she was on the mend, a trivial infection snuffed her out and the light of magic threatened to go out with her.

Funerals are such inadequate things. Kate's family organised the service and Vincent Melchior and his crowd gave the friends' orations. They all took charge of her until Paul felt that she was someone he had never known. The two of them had only ever existed in a corner of one another's lives, hardly bothering about what lay beyond. Now she belonged to them. And he would go on, like a mental patient, listening for footsteps on the stairs, or scanning the crowd in every London street, for a the cut of her coat, or the way her hair bobbed as she turned and laughed at him. It would be so tempting to believe that a drop of Dippel's oil could bring her back to life. He felt anatomised by grief as though his heart lay open on a slab, a candidate for any experiment which might effect a transfer of souls. Such thoughts were undoubtedly heresy. Anathema to any reasonable man. But reason had never been part of what they shared.

He returned to Kew alone and closed the door.

Night after night he sat up with his books, forgot to eat and watched the living shadows come and go. He would fall asleep at his desk and when day broke, stiff and stupid, stumble into work.

Friends tried to offer advice, but what use had he for consolation? He did not wish to be cured. He wished to recover even an illusion - a spectre of the love that he had lost. One night, as he slept, he sensed the rustle of something pass between him and the window. The smoke from the incense-burner stirred as though a figure had walked by.

Another night he saw a light, like a nacreous will-o'-the-wisp, dancing in the corner of the room.

The following evening, he made a pot of tea - Sencha Sakura - sweet cherry blossom - her favourite. He placed new incense in the Minka-House koro and fixed his mind upon it. Here before him in miniature was a deep verandah like the one at Kew where they had hidden from rain, one purple afternoon. Here would be the interior, smelling of thatch just as it had done the day when they had quarrelled so lightly about life after death. She said there was no such thing - that life consisted only of random moments, like stars in the sky. He had quoted his theologians then. Now he had to admit, that their pronouncements seemed meaningless. When sleep came he was conscious still, conscious enough to know that someone had entered the room and blown the lantern out.

It was a young woman wearing a white kimono, fastened right over left, which meant that she was dead. Her pale face glimmered against black hair, combed straight from a central parting and glossy as lacquered wood - her eyebrows plucked - hands held ahead like a somnambulist, eloquently poised above the teapot. Her lower half was missing, as one would expect, who knew anything about Japanese ghosts. She did not speak. She did not raise her eyes. And soon his dream moved on and she was gone.

Several days elapsed before he saw her again.

He was drowsing at his desk when a hand shook him gently by the shoulder. He lifted his head to find his tea bowl steaming. The girl in white was there. She bowed and back away, inviting him to drink.

How did one address a dead young woman in Japanese? What were the appropriate forms of etiquette? He hid his embarrassment behind a smile, sipped the tea and found that it loosened his tongue:

"Who are you and what are you doing here?"

She was unable to answer him but she bowed towards the diminutive incense-burner.

"That?"

A nod confirmed the improbability.

How tired he felt! The dark reclaimed him, but when he woke and thought about it later, he could not tell whether the apparition faded, or he merely lost the power to see it.

Gradually, he came to expect her visits. Each night he prepared a careful welcome for her. Each night she inched a little closer to his world. The skirts of her kimono materialised first, then her feet and the wooden clogs she wore. The more he could concentrate his mind the more she seemed to recover life and breath. He would not go so far as to say he enjoyed the game they played, but the promise of seeing her sustained him through his grief. One day he was alarmed to see her cry.

"What's the matter?" he asked. "Have I offended you?"

She immediately hid her face behind her sleeve. When next she looked at him her expression was calm.

She dipped her hair in the bitter dregs of his tea and wrote a character on a sheet of paper.

Of course he could not translate what she had put. He did not need to. In dreams one does not need to have a fixed perspective. Here, there, the consciousness goes where it pleases. He instinctively knew that the character meant 'longing'.

All ghosts are victims of longing. Longing for justice, for revenge, for something that is taken away. What had she lost that was wrapped up in the smoke of the incense-burner?

The following day he bought a calligraphy brush and left it beside an open bottle of ink. In the early hours he heard her close the door. She had left a painting of a winter branch. The buds were tightly closed and underneath ran a poem in the Chinese style.

'*Longing for spring, the full moon paints these plum boughs white. How long till the blossoms open?*'

She was like a flower herself in her layers of ritual dress. A flower which had never known a spring. Had she too died young and left loved ones behind?

Another time she drew a cricket in a cage:

"*Do you still sing at my door, now that I am in a distant land?*"

87

She missed her home - her home, perhaps, in form and style just like the Minka House that was his toy. Had his incense summoned her from sleep, igniting the fire of longing in her heart?

Another night:

"*Wild geese are passing overhead. How pitiful - this straggler born too late to fly.*"

Did she refer to *him*, weighed down by loss? Or to Kate, caught in his memory?

He called her Kasumi - 'mist' or 'pure flower' - knowing that she was only a dream, yet willing her to life through alchemy.

He left her offerings of flowers, and little rice cakes bought from the sushi bar.

She drew bamboo spears:

"*Frogs in the bamboo garden. No telling the pain in my heart.*"

Was she coming back? One day she touched his neck and her hand felt warm.

He left her a comb.

She put it in her hair but her poem was even sadder than before:

"*Chasing fallen petals, you have lost the spring.*"

With her hair swept up, she bustled about the room, tidying and rearranging things. But something had happened. She had mysteriously aged and he could no longer recognise the cherry-blossom wraith she had been at first. Once she spilt his tea and soaked a precious volume of Erasmus. She made him nervous. Hid his underwear. Presents no longer seemed to interest her and, feeling at the mercy of his dreams, he soon found sleep itself a thing to dread. As for the scent of sandalwood - it sickened him and yet he could not let her go.

Her last poem was scratched on the fly-leaf of a book:

"*Dreaming of moonlight the moth flies into the flame. Beware when you drink with demons.*"

He lifted his head to meet a ghastly sight. Kasumi stood before him in her shroud, her hair dishevelled, her hands powdered with ash as though she had been to a funeral. She held a fan before her face and when she removed the fan he saw with misgiving that she wore a mask, like a mask from a Japanese play - distorted with grief and rage. Slowly she began to untie the mask, and he cried out, appalled by the thought of what might be revealed. His mind convulsed with images of decay - all the abominations of Death's laboratory. He let out a scream, a howl of repudiation that made his blood recoil within his veins and seizing the incense burner hurled it in desperation at her. With his other arm he swept his desk, dashing its clutter of objects to the floor.

The ikebana flower vase, and teapot fell with such violence they shattered on the stiff tatami mat. Books and papers paddled in a flood of tea. Ink-stained petals and characters, spreading like bruises on paper rafts, lay engulfed - like wreckage carried before a tidal wave - the wreckage of his own delirium.

And he was drowning too. It felt an impossible age before he came up fighting for air. The room was quiet. Released from attachment to the home which was never hers, Kasumi had disappeared.

Stumbling to the window he wrenched the curtains back and there, in the Prussian-blue light that prefigures day, were the familiar rooftops of the world beyond; the birds just finding their voices; the garden trees whispering in summer leaf. Could it be that whole seasons had passed him by while he had slept?

Soon there would be the sound of traffic; people's footsteps in the street - simple ordinary things. How miraculous - a new beginning.

He wouldn't go to work. He would telephone and tell them he was not himself today. He would take a walk. Go out and see the world. He had a sudden thirst for colour and light, for green and sappy, living things. He would take himself to the Botanic Gardens and breathe beneath the trees. He might even go to the Minka House and say goodbye... A spontaneous vision arose of the deep thatch piled with snow. A row of icicles hung from the eaves on the sunny side and a half-melted layer of snow crusted the leaves of the stiff bamboos. There stood Kate in the doorway, wearing her russet coat and now he could see her face. Yes, he would go early and have the place to himself. Clear up first. There was such a mess on the floor. These things, once beautiful and fresh, had blown into his life like so much fleeting spin-drift. Now they had lost their bloom and he, a lover of ancient, desiccated things, his books and manuscripts, the armature of thought made permanent in ink, he suddenly saw them, like a litter of dead leaves. Love is not intellectual. Love beats its wings to death at the windows of eternity. He needed to blow the dust away. He saw that now.

But at the bamboo garden there was no chance to perform a private ritual. The place was thronged with people, mostly Japanese, all chattering and taking photographs. And the beautiful, pure bamboos were beribboned all over with brightly coloured tags. The Minka House itself, was in holiday mood, festooned with pink and orange lanterns, their streamers waving, like outlandish jellyfish.

"What's going on?" he asked in bewilderment and a young girl who was helping children to write at a white-draped trestle table looked up at him.

"Tanabata," she replied. She spoke English in the halting style of a recent arrival, punctuating her words with nods and smiles. Despite her best intentions, her 'l's and 'r's blended into the liquid phoneme she trusted from her own language, which added a note of charm: "Welcome to Japanese Star Festival."

"What is that?"

"Is a Japanese custom. Every year we - aan - celebrate - aan - traditional folk tale. It's a lot of fun. You can write a message. Whatever your heart desires. Write it and tie on the bamboo. Is like you make a wish for your life - for the year. Maybe you want new mobile phone!" she giggled.

"But why - why now?" he persisted, thinking how the English usually made their wishes at Christmas-time.

"Is a Festival for - nnn - star-lovers. She is one star - nnn - we call her Orihime - sewing girl. She is weaving Amanogawa. How you say? A long river of stars." Her arm described a rainbow overhead.

"The Milky Way?"

She nodded. "Her lover is - aan - star cow-boy - Hikoboshi. He has to guide the other stars. So when they meet, they fall in love and get married. But - nnn - it's not so good because they forget to do their work. So she is not weaving and he does not look after his cows. They wander away - get - aah - lost - in the sky." The pauses

90

made a musical subtext to her story. "Her father - he says - you cannot be together. You must go back to work. So they are very sad, but - aah - for some days every year – their paths come close and so for short time they are happy again. Then we can make wishes to them. In the old days, girls asked Orihime to help with their sewing and boys asked Hikoboshi to help with their writing, but it's all different now. You can ask anything. At the end of Tanabata the wishes go on - nnn - big fire so they can rise up to heaven. There will soon be a play - over there - to show the story. Would you like a card?"

"Thank you," for some ridiculous reason he felt he wanted to bow. "I would like one very much. You have been so kind."

She giggled again: "You can write on this table. Good Luck!"

The small children round him were solemnly penning their wishes. In the Gardens beyond he could hear the squawk of the parakeets, flocking from tree to tree. They were exotics, like the Tanabata tags, bright and loud. From the house came the sound of someone plucking a koto. Sadness, gaiety. There must have been another performance taking place inside.

What should he write on this red and dead-leaf yellow day? Everything had changed and yet it was the same. Light. Dark. Life. Death. There is an entire dimension in a word - vast skies of meaning between word and word and reactant boundaries where new ideas are born. That an idea might flood the consciousness without ever having a word of its own, had not occurred to him, but the Impressionists had learnt that ghost colours appeared between primary spots on a canvas and Hokusai had painted trees without having a word for green. With the gracefulness of a Geisha his heart had turned full circle and he felt ready to live again. Chagall, the great colourist, maintained that colours were the friends of their neighbours and the lovers of their opposites. And if anyone, the Japanese knew about that. Perhaps all opposites were lovers, like Fuji with its ice cap and its molten heart. And all lovers necessarily at odds. It took a particular kind of heresy to suggest as much but he felt drawn to the idea. After all he and his love had never deferred to convention. Loving the void which held her now intensified the kimono-coloured world which hid her from sight.

This way he could let the living moment go and know that nothing was lost.

"*No need to seek for you,*" he wrote. "*Because of you my world is a river of stars.*"

The Chenoo

For Richard Alford
One-time Captain of the
'Delmas Bougainville'

The Chenoo

Though he had been a seaman all his life, working his way through the ranks from Sea Cadet to Second Mate, Daniel Creel had never believed in the notion of an unlucky ship. Tragic ships there had been without question and one could never pass an iceberg without thinking of the *Titanic*. But the wreck of *Titanic* had nothing to do with Fate. It came of human pride and error - the one always leading to the other. In the waters Creel was bound for, the talk would be of the *Mont Blanc*, for no ship was ever marked for doom, as she was, and when she went up with her cargo of benzene and dynamite, that black day in 1917, she took half the port of Halifax with her. Yet the *Mont Blanc* was a good ship, with a good crew - and many other vessels carried high explosives at sea without mishap - only they say the pilot misdirected her as she was entering The Narrows. That however, was not what Marston meant, he said, when he used the word 'unlucky'.

This tramp ship Creel had joined had been dogged by bad weather all the way from Mexico. On his first evening he was invited to the Captain's cabin along with Marston, the Chief Mate, and Billy Benleven for a game of cards. It was something of a passion with Captain Rogers whenever they were in port. At each subsequent stop along the eastern seaboard, the business of the day being done, they had come together for Bridge and now here they were, berthed at New York, with a fresh cargo safely on board, ready to leave in the morning. They had got one hand into their second rubber, when Marston began that provocative talk which always ended with a battle of words and Billy Benleven walking out. Marston was a burly, red-faced fellow. Blue eyes. Flat cheek bones like a Slav, though his people, he claimed, hailed from Iceland. Born sailors. He had a slow, sly wit and liked to drop a word here and there and watch it do its work, with his blue eyes unblinking, a ghost of a smile hovering round his mouth. He had worked on the *Prospect* before, years before, and he liked to let everyone know it. He stubbed out his cigarette and played the two of spades.

"Luck is not an event. Luck is an energy field. When I say a ship is unlucky, I mean it has an atmosphere which those on board cannot help but draw in with every breath; something which infects the minds of the Captain and crew - which makes the hairs prickle down men's backs, and drives them to deeds they may not even live to regret."

"Give over, man!" said Benleven, who was a Christian and resented such talk.

Marston shrugged. "I've seen it at work," he persisted.

"Yes and you've seen the Ancient Mariner too, no doubt!" said the Captain

"The *what*?"

"The Ghost ship? Life-in-Death?"

Marston was not a reading man and he missed the allusion. But he fell silent for a while, mulling over the phrase and when he spoke again it was with renewed animation.

"That's it exactly. Life-in-Death. I see the signs all around us. Why else is Daniel here?" He spread his arms and threw himself back in his chair."

"He's here because our Second Mate had a seizure at Manzanilla and had to be invalided off."

"Just as you were coming into port."

"Well, what of it?"

"Just after the harbour pilot came on board."

"These things can happen."

"Oh, indeed they can. And they will again - you mark my words."

"Spit it out, then," grumbled Benleven. "And get on with the game, or I'm going to bed. *Why* is this ship unlucky?"

Marston fixed them all with his eye and ran his tongue round his lips. "Like I told you before, my grandfather's folk were fishermen from Iceland. The Icelanders were the ones for poetry - poetry and legends. The legends got from Iceland to Greenland. And from Greenland to Nova Scotia. The Mikmaq tell the same stories my grandfather told. Lived with the same dangers. Hunters

96

and seafolk, they huddled against the same winds, froze in the same frosts, feared the same demons of the North. And the worst demon of the Mikmaq is the Chenoo - a cannibal ice-monster which was once a man that had committed a terrible crime. An evil spirit can possess one's soul and turn one's heart to ice. The very cry of the Chenoo is enough to kill a man." His audience being captive now, he spread himself in his chair and relaxed his pace.

"Ever heard of Spelman?"

Spelman had been a boatswain on the *Prospect* twenty years before. He was an old-school seaman. A stickler for the rules. Weren't all boatswains? Beneath his barnacled exterior lay a decent man of sorts but there was one thing he could not stick and that was the whiff of privilege. To the deck crew he had always been tough but fair, until the graduate came aboard. University toff. A blond-haired, white-fingered pen-pusher. Father went to school with someone in the Admiralty. Julian Miles-Pomfret, would you believe? Was that a name for an A.B., I ask you? Well, the very sight of the boy, put Spelman's hackles up. And the more the lad tried to make himself agreeable, the more the boatswain loathed him. Perhaps he thought he could provoke him into some show of mettle. Was he looking for a rebuff? Perhaps he thought he would make a man of him. He laid into him that's for sure. Gave him the rottenest jobs. Taunted him. Bullied him when no one was looking. Miles-Pomfret, like the gentleman he was, took it all on the chin. Spelman redoubled his efforts. He suggested vile things. Insinuated this and that. Asked him why he didn't do the decent thing and make an appointment with his Maker. One day when they were in port - Manzanilla, as it happens - Julian had been sent to re-paint the Plimsoll line. One minute he was there in his little boat, bobbing beside the hull. The next, his boat was empty. To all appearances, the graduate had jumped ship. Well, that caused a to-do. No one on shore had seen hide or hair of him and of course he didn't have his papers with him, so it was hard to imagine how he would get by on land. They made a search of the harbour, just in case there had been foul play, or some unfortunate accident, but nothing at all was found. The Captain accepted the unpleasant duty of notifying the Company and stemming such

97

rumours as were running rife on board. Through all of which Spelman kept his head well down. And it wasn't till they weighed anchor that the body came to light. The poor boy had fallen in and somehow got entangled with the chain. Ouph! It was a bad business and it left a something inexplicable behind...

"Wasn't there an enquiry?" asked Creel.

"Oh, they found a note to a girlfriend. Broken heart. That was the end of the story."

"And you stayed quiet?"

"What did I know? I was Spelman's replacement. Spelman went off his chump."

"Well, there's no bullying on my ship. Or any ship these days," said Captain Rogers. "The rules are clear on that. And all you've got is supposition and we all know where that can lead. Play your card and do us all a favour and shut up."

No more was said about luck that night, but the story had wormed its way into Creel's sub-conscious, dredging up questions from the sea-bed of his mind. A few days later, as they were changing watch, he nailed Marston and broached the theme again.

"You said he went off his chump," he said. "That boatswain, Spelman. Was it guilt, or what?"

Marston smiled his slow smile and put his head on one side.

"You're hooked now, aren't you? Like I told you, it's *in the air*. Chap before you was just the same. It wasn't guilt. Spelman didn't think himself to blame. It was the ship."

"*This* ship?"

"*Any* ship. Every man is a ship to himself. Something coming out of his own heart can drive him over the edge. The natives along this coast know that all right. It's the silence, the dark of the North. A man has to live with his heart up here. Spelman started seeing things, hearing things each time they put in to port." He let his words settle, then folded his arms and leaning forward, put his weight on his toes. "The Captain hit it right on the head the other night. Life-in-Death - have you heard of it? The kind of madness that leads to disaster at sea?"

"Can't say that I have."

"Have you heard of ship's graveyards, then? Ghost fleets?"

Creel shrugged, feeling uncomfortable and Marston began again:

"They're all around us here. There's that place on the Potomac River, full of the rotten bodies of old wrecks. Hundreds of them there are, all weeded over and full of bird's nests and goggle-eyed fish. They go back to the Civil War some of them. Then there's the fleet in the Hudson River - freighters mothballed after the war and used as silos for grain when they got too old. My cousin once looked into it all. Took aerial photographs. You can see the vessels lined up, like sardines in a tin. Sure sometimes in the early days they came and went. But do you know? There's one, he insists, that can't be accounted for. A white ship that doesn't appear on the official lists. Sometimes it's there. Sometimes it isn't. A ghost ship, that takes off on its own. And what's its purpose I'd like to know? And who would man a ship like that? Who but the dead? With their own deadly purpose?"

Creel began to laugh, but Marston gripped him by the lapel. "No joke! I'm telling you. There is a natural law whereby like sticks to like. They say the spirit of man who's drowned can only rest when it has marked the sea's next victim. Marston *saw* that ship. There can be little doubt of that. It dogged him from Halifax to Rejkavik and on to Rotterdam. He doubled back across the Atlantic and when he got to the States it was waiting for him there. At Halifax, Nova Scotia, it basked alongside, like a whale. And when the request went out for a harbour pilot, something unspeakable came aboard. Something smelling of rotten fish. Something which left a tangle of weed on the pilot's ladder and a pool of filthy water on the deck. And the Apprentice on duty got away, but he never went to sea again. And Spelman, who saw the scuffle, and watched the abomination slide back into the sea - Spelman lost his wits. He took himself down to the bilges and when they found him he was gibbering like a fool about frost-giants and ravening cannibals with hearts of ice. That's when I got my papers to take over. I've seen nothing myself, but I tell you it's not finished yet. After all these years, there's still an unsavoury stink in the air."

After that interview, Creel did not want to know anything more. He felt distinctly uneasy about the fate of his own predecessor. Had *he* succumbed to Marston's mischief-making? Frightened himself out of his wits? For once he thought Billy Benleven was right - there were things better left unsaid. Thoughts and feelings better left unacknowledged. He had no intention of giving way to them, but all the same...

South of Cape Sable they ran into Newfoundland fog - the thick, impenetrable fret this coast was famed for. Diaphone foghorns, with their melancholy, sinking cry, were sounding from lighthouse to lighthouse along the coast. Now passing ships added their warning blasts. This weather would slow things up, which was maybe all to the good. With any luck his watch would be over before they reached Chebucto Head.

But Marston had not done with his meddling yet. On his way to his cabin he spotted the Chief Engineer.

"Billy - eh, Billy. Have you seen how twitchy the deck crew are up there?"

"What's the matter with you now?" barked Billy.

"I'm just telling you, man. If ever there was a time for prayers, now's your moment. Put in a word for us."

"You're a blithering idiot, Marston - and a menace into the bargain. Now clear off out of it. I've got things to do."

"Don't say I didn't warn you." Marston whined. "I've tried to tell you all. That Rogers is the same. Thinks he knows it all. And I admit he's pretty good. But it isn't a question of competence, is it, in the end? Not when you're coming into port."

"What in Heaven's name are you on about?"

"It's a matter of trust, of course. '*To pilot's advice and captain's orders*' remember? That's what it says in the Manual. He'll take the rap for whatever happens then."

"Well my trust is in a higher Captain."

"So - offer a prayer for us. The *Prospect* may just need all the help she can get."

Sea Fog. So cold, it lingered like a corpse's touch, imparting a clammy feel to everything. Water droplets collected on the deck-rails, beaded the beards of the crew, misted the instrument dials, seeped into every pore. As the anchor chain rolled out, Daniel Creel stood fast at the wheel. The message might be sent at any moment now, requesting a pilot to take the vessel in. In this whiteness there would be no sight of shore. The world was reduced to shadow play where vague shapes laboured at mysterious tasks. Far up at the fo'c'sle, the ship's bell began to sound - an urgent ringing to which a gong replied way down on the poop. In a minute or less these signals came again, so the ship felt like some creature, communing in distress. He found himself counting the sounds and intervals. They would be preparing the pilot ladder, checking each thing with clockwork efficiency. How comforting the regulations were! How heartening to feel the ship throbbing in suspense, like a living body, responsive through each dial and gauge. Bell... Gong... Pause. Bell... Gong. The pilot would guide them. Pilots were a breed apart, famous for their navigating skill. Bell... Gong... Pause. Bell... Gong... And then there would be time ashore and he'd write to his mother and... God have mercy, what was *that*? Over to starboard the wall of fog gave way and a vast shape heaved into view. Drifting right alongside it was - a white hull with gaping holes in its side, coming so close a collision seemed unavoidable. There had been no signal to warn of its approach. What were the maniacs playing at? Couldn't they hear there was a ship at anchor here? Hadn't they got a radio? He braced himself, checked his bearings and peered ahead once more. But now the mist closed in. There was nothing more to be seen. And whatever should he do? Raise the alarm? Or let his intelligence pacify his heart. Phantom sightings were common in fog as every mariner knew. Who had not seen spectre ships at some time or another, inverted in the sky? - the sister images of ships sailing at sea... Flying Dutchmen... Floating islands? Ghastly shadows projected by the sun? Slowly his senses, numbed by anxiety, resumed their normal function. Someone had come aboard.

Up on the bridge ahead he clearly saw the Captain and another figure too, a stalwart figure briskly shaking his hand. And the bell rang out again. All would be well. The pilot had come aboard and in a little while his instructions would start coming through. How tired he was. He had missed the sound of the gong. The men on the bridge wings moved like silent ghosts. Did they hear it? All he heard was the thump of his pulse as the tide of his fear receded and a sound he could not at first identify - the slap of some heavy object hauling itself along on the deck behind. Before he could figure out what it was, something terrible trapped his hand in a vice-like grip. Cold as jellied eels it felt, this mass of muscular wetness which had slithered up behind him and the stink of fish came with it and whatever it was, it closed fast over the wheel and spun it round and Daniel was utterly powerless to resist it. At that very moment, quite without warning, the propellers roared into action...

That was an unlucky day for the *Prospect*. The investigators found that she had been, in any case, a skeleton ship. More rust than steel. Should have been pensioned off many years before. She struck some unknown object and immediately took in water. By morning there was hardly any sign of her. The insurers would demand a full enquiry and salvage such cargo as was possible. Yet how the accident occurred remained a mystery and to his dying day Captain Rogers maintained he never gave the command. Daniel Creel's account confirmed the general view that long shifts in bad weather affected morale.

As for the rest of the crew? Providentially, they were all picked up by a nearby passenger ship. All except Marston, that is, who was never found. It was almost as though his spirit had already succumbed to some prior claim of the sea.

Leastways, that's how Daniel Creel put it when, as he loved to do, he teased his shipmates with a seaman's tale.

The Eye of Horus

The Eye of Horus

"I have seen the Eye of Horus when it was full in Heliopolis!
Let no harm befall me, therefore, in this land,"

The Egyptian Book of the Dead
Chapter 125

Sir Laurence Aylmer cut a charismatic figure, lithe, handsome and rakishly debonair. As Director of Egyptology at the Montague Institute, he had, virtually single-handed, given a new face to archaeology. He was the first to accomplish public stunts for his dusty branch of learning, lying in mummy-cloth in his own bespoke sarcophagus and rafting down the Nile, with a golden sun on his head. For all this tomfoolery, he was considered a world authority on the religion of Ancient Egypt. Indeed, amongst his many claims to fame, his work on the Temple of Horus at Nekhen remained unsurpassed, furnishing him with an endless stream of papers, lectures, and books, not to mention five university fellowships and a knighthood.

His career had been forged through a chain of happy accidents. An indolent youth from public school, with a gift for cartography, he was drafted to Egypt during the Suez Crisis, met Andrew Montfort and accompanied him on a trip to the Lower Nile. Astonished and enchanted by the antiquities they discovered, and in particular by the finds at The Red Mound, he promptly contracted dysentery and was invalided home. An early discharge and a place at Cambridge followed. And it was here that he established a reputation as a heart-breaker and libertine. His drinking parties were notorious; and he counted foreign princes among his friends.

At the tender age of twenty-nine he landed the post of Director - 'The Job', as it became known to his circle - and from that day forward, Hampstead's gothic monstrosity the Montague Institute

105

lost its reputation as a repository for fakes and black market booty and joined the ranks of the world's best-loved museums. Exotic, idiosyncratic, he himself matched the artefacts within. And neither was ever very far from scandal. His eye for the ladies was common knowledge. Pretty women who wanted to get on, could always avail themselves of his open door. He found them jobs in TV and junior lectureships. He was generous to a fault. Anyone ugly would have to fend for themselves, as Marion Denbigh Ph.D., discovered to her cost.

She was thirty years younger, a formidable candidate with a doctorate in Coptic Studies and a Lancashire accent. She was also a feminist, and though she did not go so far as to shave her head for 'Peace', she cropped her hair because it was practical and warned male colleagues not to trifle with her. She had decided views about the Empire. And she believed that merit alone should reap reward. It was small wonder, then, that she took the Director for a natural enemy.

One look at her plain figure was enough to turn him against her. At a meeting of the Trustees he behaved in his usual regrettable manner. Patronising and sarcastic, he called her 'Ms. Denbigh' a dozen times if he did so once, knowing her actual qualifications rivalled his. The post in question being a junior one, she was over-qualified and he certainly did not want to have her beady eye scrutinising his every move. He voted in favour of a willowy girl from Esher whose father had friends at the Cairo Embassy. Such connections always proved so invaluable! He did not bother to attend the interviews but here he made a serious mistake. Ms. Denbigh put up such a show of strength, the selection panel, visibly impressed, took the audacious step of offering her the job and once she was installed, the Director found, to his infinite dismay, it was impossible to dislodge her.

Clinging on, tight as a tick, she provoked a constant irritation beneath his skin. And so began an undeclared state of war, which grew until it threatened to engulf the Institute. At first he tried to shrug the matter off and after whiskies at his club, would take refuge behind a barrage of wit. His particular subject being Egyptian sorcery, he knew that in incantation the naming of things gives one a certain power over them. As though to put this to the test, he composed an entire lexicon of names for Marion Denbigh. Most connected her with cramps and tummy-ache, perhaps because of her own sour face or because she gave others 'the pip', or then again, because that was what he wished upon her. By extension of this schoolboy logic, she also appeared as 'Nasty Nanny', administering purges and taking his toys away. But his favourite epithet by far was 'Apep', the cosmic snake of the Underworld which swallowed the sun at night. Moreover, 'Apep' was close enough to 'apepsia' to suggest that she would put one off one's food. Such puerile spite achieved no practical end but it afforded him relief. She treated him as though he was invisible and subtly began to instigate reform.

I mentioned that the Institute was 'gothic'. In fact it resembled a Piranesi prison with turret excrudescences and pillared balconies in brick and stone. Sir Lionel Montague had had a hand in the design, intending it as a final resting place for himself and his personal collection. The labyrinths within were said to be inspired by the passage structures of the Pyramids. Certainly they were dark and incommodious. In the end, he was decently buried elsewhere, but his collection being too important to ignore, the place was promptly opened to the public. They called it the Hampstead Hallucination and so it seemed when looming eerily out of a London fog. Inside, the brown-panelled corridors formed a mahogany maze, with flickering gas lights, whipcord carpeting and a most peculiar smell. But it offered a cosy refuge when the weather was cold and the great houses of Hampstead, with their pianos and libraries, drew their curtains shut. The statues and amphorae dwelt among cast-iron radiators almost as monolithic as they. And there was a singular satisfaction in passing from chamber to chamber, letting the heavy doors with their frosted glass swing back upon their hinges to bury one ever deeper in the bowels of Time. Little had changed there for a hundred years, but change was coming fast.

First to go were the Director's cigars and the thick blue cloud of smoke which choked his office. Then his Greek kebabs and wine, imported from a taverna across the road. The smell, Denbigh insisted, leached into the gallery, upsetting the visitors.

He became more reckless. She more determined.

Next, in line was the photocopier. Quite apart from the fact that the photocopier room, being small and intimate, provided the perfect place for his 'casual indiscretions', it encouraged waste of paper.

Next, the Ladies' Lavatories...

The entire building was dingy, dusty and full of draughts. What it needed was complete refurbishment... In her junior capacity she had no actual power but she worked on others, and catalysed change through them.

He moved her into a small back office above the drains. *She* called in Health and Safety and had the room condemned.

Mean and despotic, he promoted others over her head, shelved her projects, withheld access to vital resources, tried, by whatever means to humiliate her. She, finding the Trustees deaf to all complaints, bided her time and began to keep a diary.

She had the Director in her sights and one day, she knew, she would enjoy revenge.

Did she find him one day with a student on his knee? Did she come across receipts for unofficial loans? Did dubious delegations from a Dr. Amun Khan come and go with impunity and rifle through the collection as they pleased, while the Director still refused to let officials from the antiquities department in Thebes so much as touch his Middle Kingdom mummy?

Only once had she confronted him face to face. She, short and fiercely bespectacled. He semi-recumbent at his desk, toying with a silver paper-knife, his lean face full of hungry interest. She had lost her self-possession, listing a litany of his faults, and ending with the bitter observation that he behaved as though he were a Pharaoh, above the law. He used the Museum as his palace and everything in it, as tribute for his personal use, including the female staff.

He raised an eyebrow.

"Virgins, you mean? What a delicious thought. And are you offering yourself, my dear? I'm afraid it won't do you know. There are limits even for Pharaohs."

After that she held her tongue, but she watched him like a raptor. One day he would grow old, miss a step, and she would be ready to pin him on the sand. She owed it to her sex, her class, to her profession. There was no personal enmity, she argued to herself... Oh but there was! A murderous loathing. And when she was sent to number bones in the mouldiest wing of the basement, or bring up tea for the curators' meetings, she promised herself that when she next caught him bending she would puncture his posterior with that hawk-headed paper-knife and he would not sit down again for a month!

At any rate, the happy-go-lucky style of the Montague Institute was under sentence of death. Away went the Krona coffee jug which had stewed for so many years in the Members' Room. Away went the dusty sofas and daguerreotypes of Sir Lionel Montague in his solar topee. A new, accountable world opened cupboards, went through files, installed hydrometers. The Director shuffled a little further into his corner and obscured himself in clouds of secrecy. His lunches took longer and longer; his contacts grew more and more questionable. But few could doubt that it was his personal flair which still accounted for the success of every enterprise the Institute undertook. Rotten inside he may have been, but his gilded mask drew crowds.

His latest stunt was to recreate a tomb beside the Nile at the moment of its discovery. Burials had been found at this particular site a hundred years before with painted cedar coffins similar to the one Lord Montague acquired on his rapacious travels through the region.

Visitors would stumble along ill-lit passageways, gradually descending to the chamber where, amongst a litter of figurines and shards of broken pots, the dazzling casket lay. The walls were flooded with golden light. Processions of fresco figures marched in rows, flanking the deceased. Overhead, a yawning rift in the roof, occasioned by an earthquake, threatened imminent collapse. An uproar ensued over public safety, which the Director overruled, doing a deal with an undisclosed insurer to cover all liabilities. The row was all he needed to create a national sensation and the queues spilled out in crocodiles onto Fitzjohn's Avenue.

At night, when Marion Denbigh went down to turn off the lights, she could not help but be impressed by the eyes so beautifully painted on the coffin-side. Eyes for the dead. Wedjat Eyes with the hawk-face tear-drop of the God Horus to let the dead see out. She could not prevent a frisson, a sense that the mummy wrapped inside, reclining with eyes aligned to those kohl-stencilled orbs, was silently watching her.

She was privately convinced that the coffin had been looted, for when archaeologists arrived at its site of origin in the early twentieth century, most of the tombs in the necropolis were empty. Lord Montague had beaten them to it some fifty years before and this casket, which he ascribed to a nomarch of his own choosing, bore the all hallmarks of Deir el Bersha - a treasury stripped of gold.

How much more fitting, she thought, for the plunder to be returned. The authorities in Egypt certainly welcomed the idea. But at the root of her push for justice lay the solitary fact that the move would be a blow to the Director. He almost worshipped that coffin. It certainly meant much more to him than the sum of its parts. It was she thought, the only thing he had ever truly loved and its loss would grieve him more than anything. She almost wondered whether he subscribed in some devotional way, to the legends about which he was such an authority. Did he *believe* in the cosmic battles, the animal-headed deities of the ancient world? Did he think of himself as their earthly incarnation? He had once contemptuously referred to her as a 'corn-grinder' - a miller of facts and figures. His view, he claimed, was visionary. Of course he knew he was a rogue - that if his heart was weighed it would be found heavy with sin. He could not help himself. But she was nonetheless intrigued by the thought that he had had an Egyptian coffin made for himself. Did he really think that after death, it would sail him through the ordeals of the underworld?

One day she met a stranger on the stairs - a dapper man with a delicate moustache, a shiny, shaven, almond-coloured head, black suit and tie, and the unmistakable scent of the orient. He smiled through neat, white teeth and waved his card. A gold charm-bracelet flashed upon his wrist and she noted an ankh and scarab amongst the charms.

"Dr. Amun Khan," he said. "I am looking for the Director."

She waved him on, watching his polished shoes mount two at a time. A leather flight bag bounced upon his back.

An unfamiliar scent tainted the air. Patchouli? Formaldehyde? "A doctor of Egyptology? My arse! More like an astrologer," she thought.

From that day forward his visits became a regular event. He and the Director would closet themselves away for hours at a time. Marion surmised that they were up to no good, but it was several years before she learned the shocking truth and in that period many things had changed.

Staff came and went at the Institute, but Marion clung on. With his advancing years, the Director's god-like mastery began to slip - it seemed the sight in his keen blue eyes was failing. He hid the matter as best he could, but 'Nanny' found him out. Now she knew it was just a matter of time. She made herself indispensable - helped him with his correspondence; typed up lecture sheets in bolder print. As he was forced to admit dependency, she gained access to his books and notes and sorted out the muddles on his computer. She found his diaries and lists of associates - she even bought birthday flowers for his women. Like Blake's 'evil worm', she nestled closer and closer while embellishing the report which would destroy him.

His sudden illness and retirement took her by surprise but now she found she had an open field. Already she had her hands on all the ropes and who could compete with her to fill his place? Who else knew so much about the Institute? Who else had so many scores to settle? The Trustees, glad to have the matter as good as decided, took the easiest course and the Director, to everyone's amazement, endorsed their choice.

Marion had the best credentials, but she... She had lost sight altogether of the work she had meant to do all those years ago when she arrived. Her Coptic studies virtually forgotten, her dream of painting in the gaps between the Pharaohs and the Christians, lost in the sands of time. Despite the sanitary inspectors and the design consultants, it seemed some spores of Institute mould had entered her system and infected her larger view.

Her first act, on promotion, was to single out those employees who had condoned the Director's ways and send them packing in a brutal purge. And she resurrected her controversial scheme of returning looted treasure. The stacks were full of crumbling specimens and modern audiences had no time for clutter. Better to have fewer effects and cut down on bacteria. And here again she found her path had been eased by her enemy's influence. A contract of permanent loan had been secretly discussed some months before and the Egyptian authorities were already designing an annexe to house the goods. What motive might have changed the Director's mind lay beyond conjecture, but wherever she turned, Marion felt his hand on all she did. Here they were, still locked in a deadly dance; parodies of themselves, as flat as figures on some Pharaonic frieze and quite unable to break the momentum of their hate.

What seems beyond doubt is that when he heard the Egyptian deal was signed, the shock of it promptly killed him. Marion Denbigh heard the news with disbelief. Her book, in serial form was due to come out in one of the major papers. Publicity had gone to press and now, just as she was about make her kill, it seemed, he slipped the net.

In his infuriating, casual way he had upstaged her again and his obituaries prefaced a stunt so extreme it electrified the nation.

Two days before the funeral, his attorney announced that he had written a new will. In it he left his entire estate to his museum successor: books, papers, substantial financial investments. His own cedar wood coffin, he bequeathed to the Institute to replace the original, now bound for overseas. Marion felt completely compromised, as she was meant to do. But worse still was to follow.

That night an intruder broke into the mortuary where the Director's body lay and stole his heart and eyes. This sparked an explosion of lurid speculation. Who was the culprit? Which of his victims could have done the deed? The public thought it was a woman, exacting revenge for misdemeanours past. Suspicion would naturally fall upon the one who had published private revelations, so she was glad she had had the sense to conceal her name.

No funeral could now take place until the police had exhausted their enquiries.

Meanwhile a horde of visitors swarmed to the Institute to see the old reprobate's coffin. Eggs were thrown and the gallery which housed it had to be closed.

Months later, with the case still unresolved, the body was finally released for burial and a quiet ceremony followed.

As she returned to the Museum, that dull November afternoon, Marion Denbigh thought she passed a familiar figure on the steps. The light was failing and when she turned she saw the street was bare. But she could have sworn that Dr. Amun Khan had brushed against her with his cashmere coat and reek of honey and myrrh.

From that unsettling moment, she suspected that some foul trick had been played. The Director had not gone. His evil influence survived in some psychokinetic form and even if she destroyed all trace of him, she could not be sure that he had not willed that too. The suspicion became a conviction and the conviction an obsession.

She ordered an immediate search of the room where he had entertained the elusive Dr. Khan. Sure enough, workmen moving a cabinet, found a large, concealed recess - something like the laboratory cupboard where that Restoration rake, the Duke of Buckingham had dabbled in alchemy. This recess, large enough to hold a bench with standing room for two, was lined with shelves and on the shelves, emitting a potent stench, dozens and dozens of freshly mummified cats.

So Amun Khan was not an astrologer, after all, but a common taxidermist and week by week he had been bringing in his bag, subjects for these macabre experiments. Even a novice in Egyptian lore would know that embalming was essential for life after death. The heart, being linked to the soul, would be left in place when other viscera were removed, so that at judgement it might win its place in paradise. But these beliefs were archaic superstitions. To subscribe to them in this modern day - to arrange for one's own mutilation and who knew what else, defied all logic. Clearly, it would be beyond the scope of any single man to snatch a corpse and find safe lodging for it. No, any thief would have to confine himself to the most essential parts...

It followed, naturally, that *Dr, Khan* must be the thief, and that he had been engaged by the Director to secure him safe passage to the Afterlife. Somewhere, she guessed, the Director's mummified eyes were gazing forth; somewhere his pickled heart, defying the laws of Time, was pleading for mercy from his pagan gods.

When she went home, those dead eyes followed her. They saw into the treacheries of her heart. Her nights became a hell-hole where she faced the demons of her own hypocrisy. By day, when she could gather her wits she began to reason: *What was more likely than that Dr. Khan had placed his spoils inside the cedar chest, eyes aligned to painted eyes, after the ancient fashion?* And if that was the case, there was no life for her until the abominations were removed. She would expose the scam for all the world to see.

A few days later there followed a grisly rite, performed by torchlight at the dead of night. Feeling their way, (the power, which supplied the alarms having been shut off), a small procession stumbled along the passage to the lower gallery. There, Marion Denbigh and four workmen, who were sworn to secrecy, opened the cabinet of strengthened glass and, placing a trolley of suitable height beside it, pulled the Director's coffin out. All held their breath and a clawing coldness gripped their hearts as the cover came away.

Inside, the searching beam picked out the golden obsequies of the dead. And... two white ping-pong balls. There was nothing else.

A paroxysm of useless rage convulsed her. Had he gone to Egypt in the other box? Was he ground to mummy dust? An itch in the nose, a parody of his own living corruption? Was he no more than a figment of her neurosis? Whichever way, he was still having his laugh, still pulling puppet strings to make her jump.

Quivering, she paid the workmen. How had it come to this? That one wickedness should so engender another? That she, who had always prided herself on her integrity and strength of mind, had been reduced shameful folly? It would not happen again. She would rise above it all - recover the self she had set out to be. It was not too late. She would forget the Director - withdraw the Diary - begin another day.

And yet... And yet however hard she tried, she could not forget his words. Corn-grinder, was she? Counting tallies and logging minutiae. Antiseptic was it, her exhibition space? Falling were they, the visitor numbers?

While he, from some glass verandah on the Nile, witnessed the golden miracle of the sun greeting eternity in its morning boat? She had a sudden longing to be released from the snake of anger which had coiled itself around her. She had a desire to leave the Institute and its scandals behind and set out for some limitless horizon. She had no more appetite for London and Gothic dust. She craved the solace of a liquid sky - a field of whispering reeds. She was feeling old already. Perhaps it was time to prepare herself, to lighten her heart and prepare for the journey ahead. How blessed to have a window of one's own - a window, say, like this beautiful eye of Horus, so calmly opening a chink between life and death. And if only she could get to the other side, then she would know that death was no longer watching her.

Somewhere, she thought, she still had the card which Dr. Khan had given her. She would ask him to visit her...

White Lead

For Michael

*

White Lead

Just after dusk, Farmer Deerfoot's daughter sat up in her bed and pointed at the wall. Her mother, who was sitting beside her, reached for water, for the child had tossed in a fever for days and her hectic cheeks and glassy eyes were proof still of the danger she was in. Since her birth four years ago, she had been her mother's constant companion. The youngest of six and the only girl after five great lumping brothers, she had grown sturdy and strong playing out in the wind.

Day after day, she trotted about the yard with her little willow basket, collecting eggs, or staggered along, in her hand-me-down wellingtons, passing the pegs, while her mother hung out her Alpine piles of laundry. And when there was work to do indoors, she curled up on the kitchen step to watch, while her brothers played their rougher games outside and helped out on the farm. Never had she been sick - not even when scarlet fever took several children in the village. But this influenza had come like the north wind, whipping round the barn and catching folk without their coats on. This one was a killer. Doctor Abberton had looked grave and mentioned croup. The cough was terrible. But worse than the cough was the gagging and silent gasping for breath. Mrs. Deerfoot burnt camphor, as she had seen her mother do when the family were sick. She even tied a ribbon round the crucifix that hung above her bed. She refused to sleep, forgot to eat, watching the crises come and go and waiting for the big one which would decide it all.

When Connie sat up with staring eyes and pointed at the picture, her mother did not know what to make of it. The room was almost dark - a solitary candle burned beside the bed and the painting, which in daylight depicted a cow beside a stream, appeared no more than a shadowy lozenge, sunk within its frame.

"There is a lady there!" said Connie, with the same conviction she might have evinced on seeing the cockerel scratching on his dungheap or the carthorse eating oats at the stable door.

"Lord have mercy on us!" cried Mrs. Deerfoot. "She's seen an angel. She is going to die!"

But Connie continued to gaze in wonderment.

"There's a white lady there," she said.

Shortly afterwards, she fell back on her pillows, and closed her eyes. Her brow broke out into beads of sweat. The hectic spots drained from her cheeks. Her ragged breaths, like waves after a storm, sank into a gentler rhythm until they were barely perceptible. She had fallen asleep.

"God be praised!" her mother cried, wiping her cheeks on her apron and stroking the child's damp hair. "Come back to us, my darling. We have so much still to do together. We haven't made the gingerbread men or iced the cake for Christmas. There's the new calf to feed and we've the chickens to pluck and you would so like playing with the feathers. Snow is coming and your brothers will make you a slide down beside the dairy and I'm sewing you a doll with a nice red dress."

Christmas could be the best and the hardest of times on the farm. Hands, chapped from carrying frozen buckets, sore lips, red ears, and toes, all itched by the kitchen fire. No scarf was thick enough, no socks warm enough to keep out the bite of the cold, but working, chopping wood, breaking ice, carting straw did a better job, keeping bodies busy and strong and appetites keen. The cows steamed in the cow-stalls; the chickens plumped out their feathers and hunched in a row on a gate. The moon silvered the tiles on the barn and washed its face in the duck pond and George Deerfoot came out from the shed where he was cleaning his oil lamps to watch the wild geese fly over.

This Christmas things seemed tougher than most. It had been a poor harvest. After the hay was cut, they had had a week of rain and the crop turned brown. The cattle would eat it but it had lost all its golden goodness. The corn fared just the same, for harvest had been beset with by thunderstorms. And now to cap it all, a beast was sickening. Despite the bravest endeavours, it was hard to keep out of debt. But farming clothes wore out. A new pair of boots, or a winter coat would put the household accounts in the red for weeks, and the tally man was always so damned cheerful, collecting his payments at the door on a Friday.

They were not alone, however. You only had to look at the faces of the villagers to know that times were hard. There had been depressions in the countryside since great-grandfather's time. People leaving the land. People selling up. Families scattered into foreign counties and always some great upheaval brewing abroad. It was 1937 and though the politicians promised peace, things didn't look any better than before.

When George Deerfoot kicked off his boots that night, his wife was peeling potatoes in the kitchen.

"How is she?" He had a hungry, hawkish look. Dark hair going grey at the temples.

Margaret dropped her knife and threw her arms round his neck.

"Sleeping! God be thanked, she's sleeping and Billy's watching with her. Come in and warm yourself. Water's boiling."

He watched her hands lift the big kettle from the hob and fill the teapot. She had been just a slip of a girl when first he courted her. Now her cheeks were threaded with red veins but he loved her just the same. It was a crying shame she had to work so hard. And if they lost the cow they would be more in debt than ever. And the rent was due in a week.

He had never told her how near they were to ruin. She had the worry of the children and somehow he could not bear to add to her cares. Just now, they had the doctor's fees to pay and maybe worse to come. If they could only get over this month, this season, this year, then they would turn the corner. The spring grass would set the cattle right again. Next year, Ned would be old enough to drive a cart on his own. And then there was the government subsidy...

At the thought that Connie might *live*, the stone which had lain on his chest all day shifted its position, so when he looked at his wife, bending over the teapot, her hands ever-so-slightly trembling with emotion, he was even less able to tell her. Let the child get up. Let Christmas pass. He'd square it somehow with the landlord. And then they'd face what was to come together.

121

"Meggie you've got to get some rest yourself."

"I'm well enough. Better to keep going. But George," she brought his tea and set it down on the table and stayed there with her hands around the saucer. "It was the strangest thing. She sat up in her bed and pointed to that picture and said: "I can see a lady there.""

"Delirious," he replied, wresting the tea away.

"George, she *saw* her! You're the one who told me about that painting. That's why we kept it, remember? Your great-aunt told you."

"Yes, and when I took it to Robert de Launey, he said there was nothing in it. It's a bit of old rubbish, done by some nobody, years ago."

"But your family has always believed that their luck was in that painting. Ever since it was at Elmford, George. Your great-aunt Lucy said."

"Great-Aunt Lucy said a deal when she'd been on the sherry."

"George I think it's a sign. You can laugh all right. But why would Connie say it? She might have heard the story but why should she invent a thing like that if she didn't really see it?"

"What are you saying? That Connie saw a ghost? Go and get some sleep Meggie afore you say something really daft."

"No - *you* wake up! I'm saying what I've told you all along - that there was more to your Aunt Lucy than you give her credit for. She gave us that painting and she bid me look after it. She said it was no ordinary painting and she'd seen the proof of it with her own eyes."

"Aunt Lucy was usually five sheets to the wind!"

"What if it was true?"

"What if she made it up? She fancied lots of things."

Margaret hung her head. "I just thought it was worth looking into. Just to see. Maybe there's money in it. And God knows we could do with money."

They dropped the subject and the boys came in and little Connie woke and rubbed her eyes. George put his rough hand on her head and smoothed the covers. He was mortally afraid of invalids, but she was his own flesh - his dearest darling - and it broke his heart to see her suffer so.

At nine o'clock, he took his hurricane lamp and made a tour of the buildings one last time. It was freezing hard on the wind; a vixen calling somewhere beyond the corn-stacks. In his mind's eye he saw his great-aunt Lucy, hobbling along on her arthritic hip, carrying the pigswill in a tub, dreaming of grandeur. They had all laughed at her. And yet she owned a locket set with pearls. And she had tiny hands, like the hands of an aristocrat, with the daintiest pink nails. Mouse paws, he used to call them. One day she slipped and scalded herself and within a month or two she was dead, taking her outlandish stories with her.

As a boy, he had enjoyed listening to them and let them fill his dreams. Then, as he grew up, he realised there was no respect to be had from consorting with Aunt Lucy. He became a practical man and put her out of his head.

The Daisy painting (every cow must have a name) had been a link to the life she left behind when she married into the Deerfoot family. It certainly had pretensions, in its massive stucco frame, though the gilt was badly chipped and the picture obscure. Perhaps it had never been very good and the paint, thickly pasted on, lay beneath a crust of Venetian varnish, so darkened with smoke, some areas had sunk completely out of sight. The painting had hung in his bedroom when he was a boy and he could imagine Lucy now, in her bonnet and black frock, sitting at the bed's foot, spinning a tale to send him off to sleep. There was a woman hidden in that picture, the old lady claimed. In his childish mind he used to think she was standing behind a tree and would one day come out. Aunt Lucy would wrinkle her nose and laugh.

"She's more secret than that!" she'd say. "She won't show herself to just anyone. We were the poor side of the family, my brothers and I - lesser cousins, who only visited Elmford once in a while. My elder brother once stopped on the stairs in front of that very picture and declared how beautiful she was. He was soon packed off to the nursery, but old Mrs. Goody remembered. Mrs. Goody was the children's nanny. She took a liking to the 'Barnford brats' as my cousin liked to call us. She would slip me biscuits from the kitchen. She never had much time for the upstairs folk - knew too much about them perhaps, for the other staff relied on her for information. '*Ears*' they called her! She could hear a whisper of gossip at fifty paces. When my poor brother died, my cousins were away at school. She was the one who let me sit in her parlour and listen to her stories."

The figure in the picture was believed to be the ghost of the first Viscountess Lullingham. Her husband had met her in Holland, in sixteen something-or-other at the English court in exile in the Hague. She was beautiful, serious, rather studious, the daughter of a wealthy churchman; he a young debauchee. After using her father's influence to further his career, he found he had no further use for his wife. Returning to England at the Restoration, he filled his house with rogues and actresses and locked the poor girl away. Childless, homesick, broken-hearted, she died, rather shockingly, of neglect. The Viscount promptly married again and spent the rest of her fortune collecting horses and art. But this portrait, said to be by Frans Hals, no less, (she was shipped off to Haarlem to sit for it, so the story goes, and the artist, penniless and not entirely sober, was said to have dashed it off in under an hour) this painting offended him, reproaching him with his former cruelty. He kept the frame, which was rather fine, and .paid a painter at court to furnish it with a new subject - a rather licentious portrait of his mistress. Guests to the house forgot the scholar bride and were beguiled instead by the scandalous Emma Lovedale - naked breasts and all! But of course, that was not *all*. As with every treachery, there came an attendant curse. It was said that Sophie Lullingham, in her Flanders lace, never really left the frame which had once been hers. A glimpse of her ghost would bring to the unwary one of two things: death (witness Lucy's consumptive brother, and the fourth Viscount who mysteriously shot himself) or else a fortune. A workhouse child, who was brought on a Sunday-treat visit, once glimpsed her and promptly inherited a foundry.

Fashions come and go. In time, Emma's offending breasts were over-daubed with roughly painted frills. Her bold, alluring eye and blushing cheek were dulled with Naples yellow and the whole became such an odious farrago, a later heir, who had a farming bent and felt disgraced by the sins of his ancestors, decided he could live with it no longer. He therefore commissioned a local hack to bury the shame beneath a country scene. This done, the thing was hung in the billiard room and later moved to a landing niche where the light was poor. And that was where Lucy's ill-fated brother saw it and where it stayed in obscurity until a new heir, the Seventh Viscount married. His London bride, wishing to renovate the house in a style that was all the rage, threw out the ornate, gilded things of the past, and replaced them with wooden screens from Morris and Co. Cupids and nymphs gave place to tapestries and mock-medieval scenes of knights and angels. Nanny Goody was sent to end her days in a cottage on the estate. Heirlooms of any value went to the bank, while the remaining trash was heaped on a great bonfire behind the kitchen garden. By chance, that was where the gardener's boy spotted the painting and, remembering Mrs. Goody's fondness for it, smuggled it to her in a barrow of wood.

"Mrs. Goody never forgot the little girl who listened to her stories," said old Aunt Lucy, smoothing her dress as though it was made of silk. "So when she died, the painting passed to me. There's more to it than meets the eye, you mark my words. One day, one of us will find a blessing in it. That's why it is in your room."

Last time they fell behind with the rent, George swallowed his pride and took the picture to a man in the village to ask an opinion. It had taken all his courage to knock at the door. The painter, Robert de Launey, R.A., had lived at Bannerman's Croft for thirty years. An eccentric figure, in a bohemian hat, he had once been much respected for historical scenes executed in the style of Augustus Egg. Standing, framed in his own doorway, his hair on end, his eyes starting wildly in his head, he had impaled his visitor with such a look and barked such furious questions at him, the farmer almost fled.

Irascible, unpredictable, de Launey was known to the village as a powerful drinker of beer and had nodded to George in passing many a time in the bar of The Farrier's Arms. Now, looking thinner, frailer, he eyed him up and down and peremptorily dismissing the painting he had brought, asked him if he would 'sit' for half a crown.

"But the real painting is underneath," stammered George. It was ploughing time and he needed every hour on the farm.

De Launey shook his head. "A woman in a white dress, you say? See this?" He picked up a tube of paint. "This is white paint. This is white lead. It's poison and it's indelible. A white dress in sixteen hundred and something? White lead. Other pigments degrade with time, but not white lead. You would see your lady shining through by now." He grabbed a rag and dipped it in turpentine. "Watch this. You can see how the fugitive greens have perished, despite the fact that the varnish is brown as treacle." As he rubbed the glaze away, a patch of tawny vegetation came to light. "Forget this picture. Come and be John the Baptist before this stuff puts me underground with painter's colic!"

George shook his head, threw on his cap, and stuffing the painting underneath his arm made his way back to the farm.

Now, leaning over the calf-pen door, he studied the cow standing humped against the wall. She had been well until this change in the weather. First it was cold and all the beets got frosted. Then it was mild and now this wind cut in from the north and the stress of calving down had brought on pneumonia. She had not eaten. Her head hung down and her sides throbbed unevenly. How pitiful she looked: eyes full of matter, her bonny, pink nose crusted over like an old earthball. She was not 'down', but he had seen animals with that look before. They did not last long once they had it. It would take a miracle to save her and if she died, he'd likely lose the calf. His thoughts strayed back to the painting.

Suppose de Launey was wrong? Suppose there *was* something in it? Suppose Aunt Lucy had heard a grain of truth before she embroidered it with her own romance? If there was a half decent painting hidden there he could raise the money for the vet to come again. He would take the picture to The Farrier's Arms and see if de Launey was there. He would sink his pride this time... and 'sit', no matter how long it took.

He stole upstairs, took the picture from its hook, and putting his finger to his lips, nodded at Billy. The boy, sitting hunched in his

126

duffle coat, was keeping watch, and doing his sums by the light of Connie's candle. George had four bob in his pocket. That would buy him beer and time to put his case. Margaret looked up from her ironing. All the housework had got behind and the boys needed shirts for school. He planted a kiss on her cheek.

"I'm doing what you asked me, Meggie," he said. "I'll be home again in an hour."

The Farrier's Arms lay at the end of the village with its sign hanging over the road. It was the working man's pub in Towton. Here was a refuge from cares of the world. Stan Hawes would come in after sweating all day at his tyring-ring and put away a pint with Leggy Matthews. There were others too, who left cold hearths or nagging wives at home to sit in the earthy dark of the public bar and breathe in tobacco smoke and ruminate over the gossip of the day. They were men of few words, most of them - wiry, leathery, shabbily-dressed - content to chew on a pipe or dream into a glass. And those who were younger, the fightable, loudly-opinionated ones, were given their head so long as the landlord could coax another ten-pence out of them.

Farmer Deerfoot stood at the door and surveyed the room. Axel Colt was there. A drinker of a different sort. His stuff was spirits - a dangerous companion but always affable.

"George!" he cried, making room by the fire. "Come and sit with me and tell me all your troubles. It has to be trouble that brings the likes of you in here!"

"Is Robert de Launey here?" asked George, glancing about him.

"He don't come no more. He's got a 'stomach', he has, from swallowing too much paint! Can't touch the liquor now."

"I came to see him."

"Well, now you're here, sit down. I'll get you a drink. You look as if you need one."

Though a voice in his head warned against it, he did as he was told and put his picture down.

"So how is life treating you? Made a mint of money yet out of your pigs?"

George gave a solemn look and drained his glass.

"My daughter's sick," he said.

A murmur of sympathy went round.

"I shouldn't be here, but I wanted to see de Launey."

Axel knew that a man in trouble is like a sheep that's got stuck in a hedge - easy pickings for any passing hungry dog.

"I tell you what," said Axel, spotting his chance. "We'll have another drink and then we'll go and knock him up."

George shook his head but he stood a round and drained his glass again.

Whisky is a powerful inducement not to go out in the cold. Once he felt the fire of it ease round his heart and radiate from there to his ribs and spine and thence to all extremities, the weight on George Deerfoot's chest vanished altogether. Unused to liquor, he attributed the inward glow to everything around him - the fire, the winking glasses, the sepia pictures which lined the walls, the red face of Walter Stiles behind the bar. All seemed like friends offering sanctuary. Even the steely persistence of Axel Colt ("Have another, George!") lost its menacing edge.

"What do you want with de Launey, then?" He nosed a little nearer.

Try as he might, George could not keep that nose away.

Gradually, the whole tale came out. How he was down on his luck. How he owed money everywhere and the cow that had calved was sick and Connie was running a fever and the man from the corn merchant's was due on Friday and there was nothing to pay him with. From there it was but a short step to Aunt Lucy and the white lady, and all the time Axel watched him, with his steely blue eyes and assiduously topped up his glass. They had been rivals for as long as they had known one another. They observed all the formalities of helping one another - lending machinery, and pitching in when the thrashing-machine came round, and they had even, on occasion, milked for one another as necessity dictated, but there was a deep distrust between them. Axel's cows had not won the butterfat prize from the dairy and one of his horses was lame. Moreover, Axel's wife was nowhere as pretty as Margaret and his son had been born disfigured. Now George had as good as laid his bosom bare, how sweet it would be to prick him just a little.

128

"I'll tell you what," says Axel, dropping his voice. "I'll lay you a bet on that picture. We'll take it to de Launey and make him scrape it clean and I say there's no Old Master in it and you say there is and whoever is right can claim a forfeit from the other."

George's head was reeling. "I've told you..."

"You don't have to pay with money. Pay with something else. You've got a horse haven't you? That big black horse. You put him down and I'll put down my Alderney cow. She went to the bull four months ago. She'll replace the one that's dying."

It is known that losers make the wildest gamblers. When you are down on your luck, it's only natural to think it must turn again. And what more can you lose if you have lost all you have already? Better to take a risk, however lunatic, than sit and do nothing at all. The cow was, George knew, a gawky thing, but she would fetch a bit at market, enough to see them maybe through till spring.

George spat upon his hand and closed the deal and the pair rolled out of The Farrier's Arms and down the frosty road, arm in arm, like a pair of long-lost brothers.

A light showed at de Launey's house, but it took Axel ten minutes' worth of hollering to bring the man to the door.

"Emergency? What are you talking about?"

"For the love of God, don't turn us away. We need your help. It's a matter of life and death."

De Launey excoriated them with a malevolent stare.

"You're drunk!" he said and began to close the door.

George interposed a hefty, hob-nailed boot: "Please Mr. de Launey. It's my Connie, d'you see. She's got the croup and she's seen the ghost in this painting. That means she's done for unless I can fetch her help. Please look at it and tell me what's in there. If there's a picture of any value I could sell it to pay for medicine..."

"We made a bargain over it," added Axel, eagerly. "But you've got the stuff to do the job. You wouldn't refuse a man when his daughter's dying?"

The pair of them, grinning like demons, leaned into the light and de Launey, who suffered from night-blindness, took some time to work out who they were. He would have turned them away but the scene made such a striking composition, he stopped, like the inveterate draughtsman that he was, to take a mental note of the way the shadows fell. Here is what he saw: a monstrous hand, in *trompe l'oeil*, gripping the doorpost; a *chiaro oscuro* nose, carved into the dark, as sharp as a weather vane; there a melting brow - a piece of pure *sfumato* - and a cheek, sunk in shadow, with a little golden window pasted on it - a perfect Rembrandt triangle! He put aside his initial irritation. Here was a gift too precious to refuse. He had been searching in vain for a subject for the Summer Exhibition... something to restore his failing reputation. These clods were pure Caravaggio. He'd lead them on a bit and see if they'd pose for him. His fingers itched already for a piece of chalk, but he must humour them first. He gradually opened the door.

"Come in. Come in!" he cried. "We're all friends in the village, eh? Can't leave you freezing on the doorstep! Don't mind your boots. Mrs. Harris can clean up in the morning."

He led the way into a hall, lined with books, and across a turkey carpet. On the far side was a low, white-painted door and then a passage to a dark-panelled dining room. The studio lay beyond, with a second entrance from the side of the house. This studio had been built out into the garden with large-paned skylights let into the roof and a glass verandah flanking its northern wall. Thick curtains had been drawn to stop the draughts. Stacks of canvases lined the walls, and, attached to the ceiling, was an ingenious hoist which could lift the artist in a cradle-chair to the tops of large-scale paintings. The place smelt of wood smoke and linseed oil. A mess of paint-soiled rags and brushes, stuck, like porcupine quills, into Chinese vases, filled a central table There were half-used tubes of paint, writhing in shallow trays, rolls of paper, rolls of canvas, boxes of chalks, glue-pots, all the paraphernalia of a busy workshop. A freestanding iron stove beside the table gave off a ring of warmth, some four foot deep, and reeked with the peculiar reek a stovepipe has when it is hot. The rest of the room lay in Siberia.

"Light!" crowed de Launey, eagerly hopping about. "We need a single source." He eyed his stupefied guests with a predatory glee, cleared a space on the table and lit an oil lamp, dropping the match on the floor. Out went the electric light and at once the room began to crawl with monstrous shadows.

"You stand there!" de Launey ordered, setting them to the left so that the lamplight cut across their faces. "Perfect. We put the picture here." The effect was worthy of a masterpiece. No matter that he could not see his hand. In drawing, it was often better not to look...

"Well, let's see what we've got."

He fetched some turpentine.

"This will get the varnish off. You roll me some balls of cotton wool and I'll make a beginning here," he positioned himself on the other side of the table. "I'll jot down notes to see how we get on." He grabbed some paper and conté crayon. And so he proceeded, dabbing at the picture and sponging away, then peering and scribbling in the shadows until he had amassed several studies and a pile of dirty swabs.

He was not exactly careful. He had a weakness in his fingers and perhaps it was for this reason, or because he was privately convinced that the painting was worthless, he did not bother to lift it from its frame. The frame itself, however, despite its poor condition, he recognised as a piece of quality and he had already determined that he would offer to purchase it as recompense for the damage he was doing.

"Now we get to the paint itself!" he observed. He would work a single patch - dig deep and see if there was any point in going on before wasting too much time.

George and Axel stood rooted, like spectators at some ghastly autopsy, while their limbs grew numb and their clouded brains cooled and congealed in solemnity.

"It's awful cold, Mister de Launey," said Axel, who was furthest from the fire.

"Eh? What? Oh, put on another log! But then come back where you were. It's most important you don't stand in my light and the oil lamp is the only way I can see the proper colours." Of course, he was lying. But the inspiration to draw was in full flow and he had to seize the moment while it lasted. Gradually, 'Daisy's' tawny green gave place to a golden ground and then a gesso size. Beneath this, more colour, at which the old man became fired up with genuine interest and doubled over his till his nose almost touched the canvas:

"Cheer up, my boys!" he cried. "We've got an eye!"

Painter's colic or not, this called for a celebration and the artist trotted off to find his brandy, leaving his visitors to stew in their own impatience. They swilled a glass all round and the work resumed.

An eye. A nose. A throat with a choker of pearls. This was undoubtedly practised brushwork, though not a master's hand.

"And she's *not* -" de Launey had donned a pair of spectacles and now glanced over the rim "She's not wearing a white dress. In fact I'm not entirely sure she's wearing a dress at all." A little scrubbing removed the satin trim and a rosy nipple obligingly appeared. "This one is not what you would call a 'lady'"

"There's more!" cried George, wringing his cap in his hands. "Beneath that one - there's another portrait there."

"Hold on. Hold on. We can't just destroy a perfectly good piece of work. This would have a certain value at auction. If you left the thing with me, I could finish the cleaning..."

"I want you to carry on!" said George, his face now menacing white. "If you don't," desperation coupled with the whisky made him bold, "I swear I'll knock you down!" His shadow towered on the wall behind him, adding to the effect and de Launey cowered a little and considered his options.

"We'll do it. We'll do it!" he adopted an appeasing tone.

"And you, boys, take another dram of this to keep yourselves warm!"

The liquor went down and de Launey now took hold of a scalpel blade.

"It's getting late. Your wives will be worrying. Let's scrape a patch and see what we can find."

The delicate glazes were unevenly pared away. By turns, the blush on a cheek, the lustre of an eye, the violet shadow beneath the collar-bone yielded to dead paint underneath. So to the pentimenti, the charcoal powder, the leprous white of the base

132

ground and at last, the rabbit skin size which had first been worked over the naked canvas.

"That's all." He laid his scalpel down as the magnitude of what he had done sank in.

"No, no - there's more!" George Deerfoot could not hold back and with his bare hands attacked the remaining paint. "She's here somewhere. The other one."

"Looks like you have lost your bet, old cock," urged Axel, laying an unwelcome arm across his back. "Go home quiet and I'll come and see you in the morning."

George brought his fist down on the table, smashing the frame.

"I've been robbed!" His face stretched and creased like a crumpled sketch, and he broke down in despair. "I've been robbed of everything. Oh God - what shall I tell, my Meggie?"

"Tell her you've been a fool. But your word's your word, all the same. Mr. de Launey - he was witness to it - weren't you, sir? You heard him. His black horse he said..."

"Take it all and go to the Devil!" George had cut his hand and now wiped the blood on his sleeve.

"I think you'd both better get out." The older man, feeling suddenly alarmed, began to push them towards the door. "Don't want any unpleasantness, do we? I'll look at your frame. Should be able to repair that for you. Might be able to give you something for it, even."

"Fortune or death - that's what she said. 'Somebody will find a blessing in it'. It's not a blessing, it's a curse! A great, bloody curse! It means a death and what shall I say to Meggie?"

"I'm sure she'll understand. Women don't take things to heart as we men do. This will all look better in the morning, mark my words. Your friend here is right. You really should go home."

George roughly repulsed the hand which patted him.

"I don't have a home..."

At this, resistance failed and the pair of rustics allowed themselves to be shuffled out into the street. Sleet cut slantwise into their faces and their boots slithered on the cobble-stones. At the corner, Axel quietly peeled away, leaving Deerfoot alone, numb and confused. His legs would not obey him. His head would

133

not steer him a course. A quiet voice warned if he did not get home, the snow, now settling fast, would finish him. Whichever way he turned, he was in a hole. How had it come to this? Ten years ago he had seemed the most promising farmer in Towton. Year on year he'd won the ploughing match. He'd snatched the best girl before all his village peers. He had the certificate about the butterfat... Now he had lost a horse. He could not plough his heavy land with just one horse. And how could he find the heart to work at all without little Connie to greet him at the gate?

He must have fallen down a dozen times before he reached the yard and finally it seemed easier to crawl along on his knees, which is how Margaret, looking out from an upstairs window, saw him.

There is something about evil which is not often said. Rakish, sinister, obscene, evil manifests itself in heroic trappings - the anti-Christ, the anathema, the void. Pantomime evil squares itself up to God with a grand gesture - a cloak across one shoulder and a hat once seen, never forgotten. But for the most part this is shadow-play. The truly terrible thing about evil is how ordinary it is - how casual. How it feeds itself on simple crumbs of selfishness and spite. How it exploits the vanities, the weaknesses of otherwise decent men when opportunity presents itself. Death is the same. No stage, no crowded room, no conflict even is needed for death to slip through the door.

George groped his way to the calf-pen where he had left his brindled cow. Make sure of her first. Hauling open the stable-door he peered inside and by the reflected light of the snow, made out her familiar form, She had gone down on her knees, head stretched upon the ground. One eye stared past him to eternity.

"Get your head up!" he yelled, grabbing handfuls of straw and piling them under her cheek. "God damn you! Get your head up and breathe!" His reason, loosed from its moorings, bobbed about like a boat at sea, but he had not yet given up. He must somehow clear her windpipe, open a way for the lungs... With a Herculean effort he wrestled with the beast, which rolled its eyes, and groaned and promptly expired. The last of her frosty breath congealed on his face.

George took the head in his arms and, rocking back and forth began to sing to it:

"Bonny lassie, will ye go, will ye go, will ye go..."

And he found something so deeply comforting and absorbing in the sound of his own voice, and he gave himself to it so completely, feeling it lift and carry him, that he was quite unprepared for the shock of a blow on his back and he reeled and gasped aloud. Behind him, in the doorway, stood a figure in white. From where he sprawled, she towered over him, dark hair, loose, eyes flaming; her long shift falling in folds to her ankles... Was it *her*? Connie's vision? And had she come for *him*? She raised one arm to strike again, with the blur of the snow whirling round her.

"George Deerfoot," cried the phantom, "you are the biggest waster God ever put upon the earth! Just when we need your help - really need it - *you* go out and get drunk and come home on your knees."

"Don't hit me Meggie!" he pleaded, covering his eyes as reality flooded in. "I was trying to act for the best."

"I've half a mind to dunk your head in the horse trough. That would sober you up and it would be no more than you deserve. Perhaps you are lucky the water's frozen, for it's only the thought of nursing you after prevents me." Her arms, strong from lifting children and heavy pans of cream, seized him and she dragged him to his feet. "You get yourself indoors. Look after the living. *That* creature's lost to the world. Have you forgotten you have a family?"

Together they stumbled back to the house and there by the range she chafed his frozen hands and tended his cuts and boiled a kettle for tea. Slowly, through the cloud of his confusion he recalled all the painful things he had done and said that night.

"It's gone, Meggie," he cried, putting his head in his hands. "It's not just the cow, or the painting. I wagered our horse as well. And now the winter milk will be short and how do we feed the calf, or pay for the doctor? And the rent is due this quarter day. I cannot farm without Trojan - and even if I could, the landlord wouldn't let me default again. We'll be turned off our land and..." he looked up with a helpless expression, "What hope can there be for Connie? I thought you were... I thought that you were *her*. Don't you see? The thing she saw..."

Margaret threw her teacloth on the table. "What's that? What's *any* of that to me? You great fool, can't you see? I thought you were dead or lost in the snow. I thought that you were hurt..." She leant against the table, with great tears streaming down her cheeks, and Billy and Charlie, who had left their beds and were sitting on the stairs with eyes dilated wide, could not tell whether she was going to hit him again or throw herself into his arms. There was a silence so long, they took their candle and crept back to their room.

"What has happened?" said George "Is she...?"

"...still sleeping. As you should be. The fever has come down. You get yourself to bed. I'll sit with her and wake you if there is a change."

At Bannerman's Croft, de Launey closed his door. It had been a mistake to touch the brandy for his insides now were griping and the nausea was not entirely physical. He felt that something unclean had pervaded the house - a spirit of ruthless ambition, which left an ugly mark on his consciousness. And he was not sure whether this thing had been dormant within him or whether it had stumbled in at the door with those simpletons George and Axel. He felt as though a crime had been committed and the canvas in the studio certainly gave that impression. In the lamplight it looked like a savage assault: a woman with no face, no heart - beauty and life expunged. Had he ever really understood either, he wondered.

In all his dealings with women he had worshipped the form, but never really bothered what lay beneath. Was it possible that *this* was the truth? That an individual could be reduced, layer by layer till nothing at all remained? A mere *onion*? And if this was so for a woman, was it the same for him? He had always maintained that he had no need for a soul; his work was his posterity. Now that he was old and his body gave daily reminders that his time on earth was brief, the world itself had lost interest in his work. Who wanted meticulous brushwork? The modern school were busy unlearning it - paring life back to its naked elements - staring into the void. And he was no longer sure that he had done enough to secure any lasting place on earth. Heaven he had never considered and it seemed too late to do so now. He would be rubbed out and he probably deserved it.

He tinkered a little with the painting, then went to bed with a half-formed resolution to make all right in the morning.

In the early hours, he was visited by a dream: he had risen and put on his dressing gown and his down-at-heel leather slippers, and, drawn by a light, made his way to the studio. He was sure he had extinguished the lamp the night before, but here was visible proof to the contrary. A golden beam lit the floorboards beneath the door and as he turned the handle the beam shot out and touched him too. Dazzled, and suddenly alarmed, he faltered in his tracks. In the centre of the room stood the table where his oil lamp burned, its naked flame glancing off the chimney glass which had been removed, and lay amidst a litter of matches. A figure, whose business of lighting the lamp had been interrupted by his arrival, turned to face him, and stood, half illumined, in the traditional manner. The folds and creases of her gown formed a dazzle of contrasting tones; one hand extended towards the light; her face, a study in painterly effects This whole apparition glowed, enfolded in shadow, both the deep and tangible darkness of the distance and the soft penumbra which paled around her head. Her eyes, gravely surprised, examined him with interest. She exhibited a beauty which made him certain he was dreaming. But for all that, she smiled and slowly beckoned to him.

He duly stumbled forward.

Now he could see that in her hand she held a tube of paint. She proffered it to him. No, 'proffered' is too slight a word. The gesture conveyed an imperiousness which the sweep of her arm confirmed, indicating the ruin of Farmer Deerfoot's painting.

Again she beckoned and nodded as though introducing him to it. She laid the paint, white lead, upon the canvas and challenged him with a look.

For the first time in his life, Robert de Launey felt lost for words. He edged around the table till the light was on his right and fumbled for his glasses. To his astonishment he found that when he put them on the vision before him vanished. When he took them off she obligingly reappeared. Now, transfixed by what he saw, he let his hands assemble, as if by memory alone, the materials of his craft. This jar here was linseed oil, this turpentine. Here were his marl-stick, palette and cotton rags. He could not see, in any case, with any practical precision. As before, he felt a rush of energy coursing through his veins - sparks in his fingers, Blake would have said - and the tremor of his hands was increased by excitement. Here were his colours, still arranged from previous day's endeavours. But to catch this now...

He could not work in his usual painstaking way. This had to be dashed off complete before the morning. Daylight would ruin it and in any case, and he might wake up and forget what he had seen.

He set to with a boldness and freedom not experienced since he was young. Time and again he lost his grip and the brush fell from his hand, dashing the canvas with random flecks of paint. Sometimes he used the wooden end like a knife or, holding the brush in his teeth, scraped with his knuckle to capture an effect. And naturally, as he worked he painted himself. His hands were streaked with colour. There was paint in his beard - for he could not resist that habit, however fatal, of twisting the bristles between his fingers and thumb. By strokes and flashes a composition took shape - the face of an angel with quiet, grey eyes; the golden coil of a ringlet; a flush of pink beneath a finger-nail. And the dazzling points of her collar and cuffs, the ribbons, tassels, and laces of her betrothal dress, all vivid as life itself...

At length, exhausted, he laid his palette down and raised his eyes, entreating permission to rest. The figure before him extended her fingers as though she would have them kissed. Then suddenly changed her mind. With a look of pure dismay, she noticed that the flesh of her arm was being eaten away by a creeping decomposition. She put a hand to her cheek to feel bare, grinning bone, and then, in an act of self-obliteration, opened her jaw. From the abyss within, it seemed, a haemorrhage of darkness extinguished her and de Launey fainted with fright and hit his head on the table.

This was how Mrs. Harris found him in the morning and, thinking he had had a seizure, called at once for the doctor.

By first light, when the cocks began to crow, the snow lay several inches thick and was falling still. Margaret Deerfoot raked out the kitchen range and put new logs on the fire. George fell out of bed after repeated shakings and threats. His head, which resounded like a drum to the slightest vibration, felt dislocated, somewhere apart from his body, but hard as he tried he could not ascertain where. His stomach also appeared to be adrift and made distressed migrations up and down, unable to find a suitable resting place. The very thought of moving about made him queasy. But out he must go for the milk lorry came at eight and the driver had a nasty temper if the churns were late.

He poked his head in at Connie's door. The child lay quiet, her hand clutching the rag that she carried for comfort.

Eight days till Christmas. If this snow went on the boys would be able to try the toboggan he had made them. He could not bring himself to think about last night. Meachum and Sons would take the cow for dog-meat. And then they would have to decide about the future. A pity, for he loved the farm - the long, low buildings, the smell of the cows, the poplars that caught the light of the evening sun. He loved coming in at night and closing the door and chopping his own firewood and lifting the children up in his brawny arms till they bumped their heads on the ceiling. He loved his wife. He loved tucking his arm under hers in bed and stroking her hair with his fingers. Many a man had never known these things. Axel's wife was a shrew and his son had a hare lip. The man had a vicious heart but who could blame him?

He took his lamp to the cow-stall and filled the wooden feed-barrow with cattle cake. The cows looked well, their flanks like rough carpets where they had licked themselves. Hauling the pails, washing and filling the churns and heaving them up onto the stollage by the gate, gradually restored a sense of rightness. By the time he returned to the house, Margaret had let the chickens out and fed the orphan calf. The kitchen smelt, as always, of sweet milk. The boys, in their school jumpers, were eating bread and jam, and kicking one another under the table and slipping scraps to the dog. In their minds they were already pelting snowballs and scuffling with classmates on the way to school. The scene before him, so familiar, seemed clear as an etching, scribed with a diamond point. George almost believed that what he saw was real. Then memory flooded in and the illusion paled. Memory revealed a betrayal of trust so great, it destroyed any belief in solid ground. Their lives, he saw, were scratched on a bubble finer than glass.

In Connie's mind, however, illusion had a validity of its own. She was sitting up in bed, in her red dressing gown, her face very pale, a white ribbon in her hair.

"Where did the picture go?" she asked.

"Daddy moved it. Will you try this for me?"

Margaret inched towards her and offered her a spoon brimming with broth.

Connie hastily retreated, buttoned her lips and screwed her eyes fast shut.

"Don't like it. It's got things on it!"

"A little bit of fat from the marrow bone. That's all. It's to make you well again. Them globules - they're little fairies, see. They're here to help you."

Connie was *not* such a fool as to fall for that.

"It's got things floating on the top. Don't like them!"

Margaret put the spoon back in the bowl. More battles. Life was nothing but battles.

"Could you eat a bit of biscuit, then?"

Connie tilted her head and squinted to see if the offer was genuine.

One glimpse of her favourite arrowroot wrought a transformation.

Now she was sitting up, with eyes and mouth wide, like a baby bird. Five minutes later she was asleep again.

Out in the yard there was an altercation.

Axel had not come for the horse himself. He had sent his cousin, the blacksmith, twice his size. But two other men were there, remonstrating with him. One was the village doctor, the other a wisp of a man in a black fedora. He was elderly, stooping and coughing under the effort of carrying an object too large for him. Resisting every offer of help, he set this object down against his leg, and made occasional dabs at a bandage which had slipped down over his eye. George came out of the house in his shirt sleeves and the row continued, the blacksmith flexing his muscles as he was wont to do and the doctor propritiating, while the shorter man hopped about like a bird on a string. At last the old fellow pulled a wad of money from his pocket and peeled off a number of notes. This had the desired effect and the blacksmith took his leave. The remaining three tramped solemnly into the house, where the parcel was laid, like a corpse on the kitchen table.

"Meggie!"

She was already at the door.

"Meggie, Mr. de Launey here has got something to show us."

"And how is your daughter, Mrs. Deerfoot?" said the doctor. Always a model of politeness, he doffed his hat, which Margaret took and laid respectfully on the dresser.

Always the same. How was it that when anyone of importance called they invariably found the washing up not done, ash in the hearth and George's old coat and boots stuck in the doorway? She mastered herself enough to say:

"She's playing up already, thank you, doctor. I reckon that's as good a sign as we can hope for."

Marvellous woman, Farmer Deerfoot's wife. Dr. Abberton smiled and nodded. "I'll be up and take a look at her in a moment. But Mr. de Launey wants to speak to you first."

The artist, in his excitement, had left his fedora on and now proceeded to unwrap what he had brought.

"After you left I was too excited to sleep. Well, sleep and I have been strangers since I don't know when, but this was different. I must confess to you that I owe you an apology. When you and Colt arrived, looking like two ruffians, I thought to myself I'd match you, like with like. I'm not the most scrupulous man, I admit. I have begged, borrowed and stolen in my time. I meant to amuse myself at your expense. I meant to let you stand in the cold while I took your likenesses down, which is common theft. And worse, I thought to crib a frame off you. You would have thought yourself rich to gain a couple of pounds and the frame you brought, I saw at once, was a genuine antique - it might have lent substance to a painting of my own...

"Still, the more I looked at the picture you brought with you, the more I felt there *was* some mystery to it. That lumpish cow in hand-scrolled gesso and gilt? The two were as unlikely a pair as you could wish to see. Though I did not believe your tale, I found myself intrigued to find out more. Then as I started work with my rags and turpentine, I discovered it was not paint and varnish at stake, but human sympathy. I had seen the torment in your face as a useable commodity and when you threatened to strike me down, I confess I was as shocked by the blankness I saw in myself as by our ruin of a perfectly decent painting. After you had gone, I knew that yours was the real undoing. I've come across old Swinton. If ever a landlord has a heart of flint... Well, by now the frame was ruined, too. As for the sketches I had made, even in my excited state I could see that they were failures - rubbish - kindling - nothing more.

"I am a dying man, I don't mind telling you. The doctor here will confirm it. My constitution is crumbling. Brain, hand, eye - the lightning reflex that was my signature - no more than a senile fumbling now. Lead poisoning, you see. There is no cure. Once I was the darling of the Royal Academy. Today, my name has become a laughing stock. Why else should I grab so desperately at one more chance to make my mark - show the young puppies what true genius is? Seeing you in the lamplight stirred me to try again. I have no other excuse for what I did.

"Polarity, you see. Light and dark, matter and void, good and evil - the essence of great art - *all* were in your faces. Polarity provides contrast, conflict, but put the two sides together and you have something new - a third concept - composition. And this synthesis is the root of harmony. The Holy Trinity. One, two, three, you see? Pythagorus and the Golden Section. And before you know it you have the Mona Lisa! Of course, I don't expect you to see. My own illuminations come so infrequently now I am hardly sure myself. Polarity is death and life - and what synthesis comes from that? An ache - a longing sweeter than life itself...

Good, evil... nothing is ever whole for long." He checked himself and returned to his narrative:

"After you left, I say, the debt I owed you weighed upon my conscience. I should never have touched that brandy. The devil was clawing my belly and banging a drum in my head, but I went back to look at the picture once again. Perhaps something could be salvaged, I thought. Now, with greater care, I stripped the remaining varnish back and wiped out the last of the cow to reveal what lay beneath. In the lamplight, the true voluptuousness of that figure could be seen - something compellingly tainted, so that even when one looked away the *sense* of corruption persisted. I had half thought to repaint the face, but this would merely have compounded one wrong with another. I could not find the heart to do it and went to bed.

"Now you yourselves must judge whether what happened next was true, or whether my own intellect made it up." He then related the events of the night. How he had, in a visionary frenzy, taken down the portrait of a ghost and woken to find Mrs. Harris shaking him. Her practical good sense averted disaster.

"That part at least is true," confirmed Doctor Abberton. "How he did not set fire to himself and the rest of the village too, is a mystery. But I *can* confirm that there's life in the old dog yet. His flesh and blood may be failing, but here he is after a fall which might have done for a stronger man. I can only deduce his head is made of wood. Apart from the cut on his brow, he has no sign of injury. No sign of concussion at all."

Ignoring the interruption, de Launey proceeded with his account. Once he had been revived with tea, and wrapped in a warming blanket, they had together examined the evidence on the table. The painting was real enough - the paint still wet, the brushes lying just as they were when he set them down. And one could tell at a glance that Frans Hals did not paint it. Was it possible that amongst his ruddy, round-faced, subjects, the Master would have set his seal to this English violet? All the same, de Launey hoped that if he had chanced to see it, he would have found some genuine merit in it. He had recognised the greatness of Van

Dyck - why not de Launey? Who knew what ghostly hand had driven his own?

With admonitions not to touch, he pulled the covers back and lifted the protective piece of board. All crowded close to see.

The subject before them returned their gaze with an even gaze of her own. Her expression was hard to read - a mixture of hope and fear. One hand reached out and tendered a sprig of myrtle. This spoke of love. But the other, clasped to her heart, as though it pained her, suggested some sadder emotion. Perhaps she knew the fate she was coming to. Her hair was swept up, in the latest fashion - a beribboned coronel with flowing curls. Her dress, gleamed, dazzling as a field of ravined snow - the whole composition had been dashed off with astonishing verve...

"This is not what you hoped for," said de Launey, pulling his beard. "Not destined *yet* for the National Gallery, but with your consent, it *will* go to London next Summer. De Launey's last piece and undoubtedly his best. I may not be there to see it sell, but I am confident it will and you shall have the money. I mean to make amends, you see. I have money and what use is it to me? I cannot take it to the Afterlife. I'll settle the payments with Swinton. *And* with the Doctor." Here he gave a considered wink at Abberton. "And I've paid off that villain, Colt. What do you say? All I ask is that you consent to be John the Baptist for me once in a while - at least until I am too far gone to draw."

Margaret stared across the room at George and George rubbed his head till his hair stood up on end. This would change everything. This would take away the gnawing fret about tomorrow. And they could have a proper Christmas. He'd go out and cut holly and fill the house with it. And they'd buy sugar mice for the children and Margaret could throw away the shoes she had patched with card and have a proper pair... And perhaps there would be an end to these difficult times. Perhaps the country would decide that it needed its farms, after all... In the midst of these plans a stray doubt crossed his mind. Would they still be happy, be true if they did not have the hardship to hold them together?

"Don't rightly know what to say," he said. "I suppose it depends on Connie. It's her lady..."

144

Doctor Abberton stepped forward. He could see the damnfool wavering.

"Enough of that. Let's ask her. I need to see that young lady in any case." They trooped upstairs and waited by the door, while Margaret went in and woke her daughter.

"Connie, the doctor's here and wants to ask a question. Sit up, nicely for him, there's a dear."

Connie blinked and, as realisation dawned, made a terrible face at her visitors.

The doctor, who was used to this kind of welcome, advanced undaunted. "Well now, you look better, miss." He snapped open his black leather bag. "No more temperatures? Say aaah!" He prodded her tongue with a wooden lolly stick. "Let's feel your pulse... And have a listen here... Cough for me. Very good. Oh, and we've got a picture to show you. Have you ever seen this beautiful lady before?"

With the thermometer still in her mouth, Connie transferred her scowl to the painting. She shook her head firmly in denial."

"So you wouldn't mind if this gentleman took her away? Excellent. Ninety-eight point four. Cough syrup when you need it. And make sure you are better by Christmas Day!"

Connie fixed the company with a resentful stare until they had left the room. But Margaret turned back.

"Connie, are you *sure*? Are you sure that wasn't the lady you saw on the wall?"

Connie shook her head. "My lady was alive." She pointed to the lozenge shape where the painting of Daisy had hung. "Look! Can't you see her? *My* lady is still there."

A Moonlight Flit

For Tina

A Moonlight Flit

Miss Purdew and Miss Barclay ran the cats' home and 'The Happy Hunting Ground' pet cemetery at the roundabout just before Lower Bleeding. Here, for a fee, owners could purchase eternal rest for their life's companions. A bloodhound funeral might cost five hundred pounds. Anything smaller than a guinea pig was entitled to the economy package: fifty pounds apiece. Rhyming memorials were extra, as were anniversary announcements in the local press. Miss Purdew and Miss Barclay walked into the village every week, wheeling a supermarket trolley of their own, which they filled with tinned cat food at the local store. The owner would announce from the doorstep:

"Look out! Here they come: the Lamp-post and the Pillar-box." Miss Barclay was long and thin, Miss Purdew round and red. They wore long cardigans and smelt of embalming fluid. They were also table-rappers and offered a counselling service for the bereaved plus séances at which the deceased could send fond messages home and make requests for donations by standing order. The chapel of rest, a portakabin, with office space and large cold-store attached, concealed the camper van where the duo lived.

Sceptics thought there was something fishy about it. And it's true, a more unlikely pair could hardly be imagined when it came to running blogs from Paradise.

Nobody knew where all the cats came from either. But suddenly there were hundreds of them, plus a goat, which occasionally ate the flowers on the graves. Miss Purdew played the electric organ, while Miss Barclay gave the address, liberally peppered with words from Omar Khayyam.

The District Council had received numerous complaints about psychic disturbances. Incoming aircraft reported unlicensed flying objects endangering life and limb, and quite in violation of local airport restrictions. To which Miss Barclay said she did not possess

149

a drone but could not control the angels. During séances, people found that their television screens went blank. The internet became unreliable. Passing sat-navs lost their signal. And customers? The strangest-looking people.

One day a body from the fraud squad raided the village shop and demanded to know where the counterfeit money was coming from. Mr. Saleh said he knew nothing about it, but he had noticed that the cash the old girls brought in had a greasy feel.

Next came the Inland Revenue. No end of year accounts had been received and demands for penalty payments had been ignored. This was just the kind of black market scam the new tax system was designed to eradicate.

The local vicar also had a deal to say and railed from his pulpit against the cemetery's false profits. He was allergic to cats, in any case, and the nightly screeching from the roundabout was enough to raise a rash on his sensitive skin.

Health and Safety had condemned the place. The local farmers saw it as a refuge for vermin.

Candida Winsomley-Belcher, M.P. called it a 'blot' on the face of England.

As for the National Park Authorities, they had no record of planning permission, no record of anything, come to that.

Miss Purdew and Miss Barclay had always been there. Their old green camper van was gently mouldering among its trees long before the current administration were out of nappies. Not that they were out of touch with the world. They were too much *in touch* with *everything*, it seemed. And they had their own vehement complaints to make about Christmas lights disrupting navigation for the spirits at night; about church bells and fireworks frightening the cats and people dicing with death on the roundabout. Debate ran hot in the parish magazine.

There were meetings, protests, and someone set fire to a broomstick in a dustbin.

Then a reputable building contractor weighed in offering a mint of money for the site.

The redoubtable spiritualists took to the air, with their own social campaign. They offered an online friendship service for lonely dogs. A one-to-one, real-time chat-line where cats could watch goldfish and budgerigars and people who had no pets could adopt a cyber companion for a day. But the last straw was a Hallowe'en promotion, offering a range of tasteless ghoulish encounters and trips to the Hereafter.

A group of militant mothers pitched their tents on the verge beside the road. The place wasn't safe for children they trumpeted. Placards waved on one side. On the other, a skull and cross bones waved defiance back. They had built a barricade of chairs and tables.

"We will *never* surrender!"Miss Barclay screamed.

"You won't take us alive!" shrieked Miss Purdew. "We've got help on the way."

The media came just in time to catch the arrival of an ancient hearse, whose driver, a cadaverous figure in top hat and veil, flourished a riding crop in the antique manner, as he swept in through the gates. The occupant within - a familiar shape beneath a pall.

Everyone stood and stared for the gates remained resolutely locked yet the hearse had disappeared amongst the trees.

Somebody called the police. A riot van, pulled up and officers armed with tazer guns piled out and began to storm the defences. First in line were the shield and helmet brigade, and they came under a hail of vegetables lobbed from the stronghold within.

The cats alone caused several casualties. But when the turnips and rotten pumpkins ceased, and the forces gained access to the inner sanctum, they found a scene of utter ruination. Here lay the wreck of the antique hearse, half in a ditch and overgrown with nettles.

The ruined Chapel beyond, with gaping windows and doors, had mushrooms the size of cauliflowers growing out of its walls. As for the camper van, encrusted with green, it had been a home to feral mice for longer than any could tell. The graveyard, comprised no more than a patch of scrub - blackened stalks of hogweed and spiny teasel waved above nettles scabbed with damp decay.

There was plenty of cats' meat, though, neatly stacked in tins on the mortuary slab. A rusted tin opener lay conveniently to hand.

151

All afternoon they stayed, sifting the evidence and taking forensic photographs. Somebody found a mysterious letter 'A' lying in a ditch.

"No wonder we couldn't find them on our records," said one detective, eager for promotion. "They were originally called 'The Happy *Haunting* Ground."

"Suppose someone done away with them?" suggested a recruit, half hoping to find a body.

"Who do you think was throwing the Brussels sprouts then?" The sergeant-in-charge, was inclined to be sarcastic. "Get on with your job, will you? They can't have got very far."

They put out a search of the surrounding area but as daylight faded they had to admit the scent was going cold.

"They've done a flit!" groaned the sergeant, his humour waning.

Then, as a hunter's moon rose above the Adur estuary, an eerie apparition glowed in the sky. Something shaped distinctly like a coffin with three figures sat astride, looped above the glistening mudflats and with a cackle, which sounded very much like laughter, and a cloud of sulphur, soared away.

"Typical!" snarled the man from the VAT. It was the following morning and he was just buttering his toast when his wife read out the newspaper headlines. "Nocturnal phenomena, my foot. They were bloody moonlighters! I almost had them. I had a premonition about that lot. Didn't I tell you they had a funny smell?"

The Magpie's Nest

A Summer School

The first of the Trudi Larsson stories...

The Larssons are a model, modern family: successful parents, clevere children, a comfortable, suburban home. Everything seems just fine until Grandfather Larsson comes to stay. Then uneasy cracks appear. Old Per brings draughts of a subversive other-world from his forest-home in Sweden and within days of his arrival the household's careful summer plans are in disarray.

While her parents fume at the disruption, ten-year-old Trudi is intrigued by Per. Why is he so secretive about his past? And where does he go when he should be asleep in his bed? And how does he contrive to know things no one has ever told him? In defiance of everyone, she sets her heart on uncovering the truth.

Gradually her safe, suburban world reveals hidden depths. Trudi finds herself on a path which will bring her face to face with her darkest fears, but by now there can be no turning back... She has already been bewitched, for Grandfather Larsson is no ordinary grandfather and his secrets are the secrets of enchantment.

Did you think that magic was child's play? Think again.

'A journey to the interior of things is an adventure for any curious mind and everything is curious for those with eyes to see.

The Beehive Cluster

A Novel for All Ages

Trudi Larsson's second adventure...

On a fragile planet with few choices left, technology promises magic solutions, but if reality can be re-mastered at the touch of a button, how can one know what is actually true? And what place is left for the old magic of the imagination?

These are questions at the heart of Rosemary Pavey's tale. For the young rebel, Trudi, they become a battleground between the mythic world of her half-Sami grandfather and the machinations of a plot to steal the blueprint of life.

Bees, stars and spindle whorls... From Inca legend to Arctic snow, the story takes a roller-coaster ride, charting landscapes invisible to the ordinary eye.

Here you will find humour, adventure, skulduggery and the breathtaking patterns of the cosmos.

Welcome to the world of The Beehive Cluster...

Hold tight, for things are not quite what they seem!

Christmas Ghosties

Tales For A Winter Night

Everything you need for a winter night's entertainment.

Nine ghost stories in the classic style, conjuring shadows from within and without...

"Call in the cat, close the doors, put another log on the fire and curl up with these tales which range from the curious to the downright spine-chilling!

From the backstreets of Brighton to the wilds of Wales, you are never far from a badly buried past, and of all the times of the year when the dead are restless, Christmas is surely the best..."

Tales include: *The Last Parcel, Grimalkin, The Horse Rider, Dooley's Bar, The Hand in the Fire and Knockings*